CHRISTMAS ON THE RIVIERA

JENNIFER BOHNET

Boldwood

First published in Great Britain in 2022 by Boldwood Books Ltd.

Copyright © Jennifer Bohnet, 2022

Cover Design by Debbie Clement Design

Cover Photography: Shutterstock

A CIP catalogue record for this book is available from the British Library.

Paperback ISBN 978-1-80426-419-5

Large Print ISBN 978-1-80426-418-8

Hardback ISBN 978-1-80426-420-1

Ebook ISBN 978-1-80426-417-1

Kindle ISBN 978-1-80426-416-4

Audio CD ISBN 978-1-80426-425-6

MP3 CD ISBN 978-1-80426-424-9

Digital audio download ISBN 978-1-80426-422-5

Boldwood Books Ltd
23 Bowerdean Street
London SW6 3TN
www.boldwoodbooks.com

'Men's courses will foreshadow certain ends, to which, if persevered in, they must lead. But if the courses are departed from, the ends will change.'

— A CHRISTMAS CAROL. CHARLES DICKENS.

1

Gabriella Jacques wasn't a fan of December. So much had gone wrong during that month in past years leaving too many days with anniversaries she couldn't help but remember, however much she wanted to forget them. Through the years she'd tried for her granddaughter, Elodie's sake, to push certain memories away during daylight but at night, they inevitably flooded her mind with sad reminders of a life she'd left behind so long ago.

Today, December 8th, was the one of those days. And the reason she was wandering around Dartmouth, the Devonshire riverside town that had become her home when she'd married Eric all those years ago, hoping the Christmas lights and atmosphere would lift her spirits and keep her thoughts occupied with other, happier, times. The town was certainly showing its festive side. Window displays had been given over to either Nativity scenes or filled with seasonal decorations. To the delight of small children, rotund snowmen, pixies and fairies surrounded a jolly Father Christmas with his sleigh full of parcels pulled by a reindeer with a flashing red nose in the large window of a pop-up toy shop. The sound of recorded carols wafted in the air as shop doors were opened and closed and strings of gold, silver and red lights were strung across the streets.

Gabriella slowed her pace as she noticed the sign indicating the 'French Christmas Market'. She'd forgotten how delighted the council had been when announcing the French theme for this year's wooden chalets in the gardens on the embankment. The smell of baked socca drifted towards her, awakening her taste buds and transporting her back to the countless times her mother had bought her a piece from the stall in Antibes market. Today would have been her mother's ninety-seventh birthday. Gabriella stood and watched the man removing the latest batch from a huge cast iron tray in a brick domed mobile wood oven. Suddenly nostalgic for the taste, the money was in her hand as he began to cut the socca into slices.

'Une tranche, s'il vous plait.'

Handing it to her with a smile, the man wished her, 'Bon appétit' as she turned away and made for a bench overlooking the inner harbour. Comfortably settled, Gabriella closed her eyes and took her first bite of the savoury chickpea pancake as she allowed happy memories to surface in her mind.

She could hear music coming from one of the stalls – French music that she'd grown up listening to. Edith Piaf singing 'La Vie en Rosé'. Charles Trenet singing 'La Mer'. Musical reminders of happier times long ago. Sitting there, listening to songs and the occasional bout of conversation in her native tongue between the stall holders, Gabriella couldn't help feeling that the atmosphere still decidedly lacked the feel of a proper French market. The socca though, had been an authentic taste of the France she still thought of as her real home.

Gabriella caught her breath as she heard the voice of Tino Rossi singing 'C'est Noël'. Her mother had loved this song and had played it over and over in December to the irritation of her father. She fingered the envelope in her pocket. Strange that such an unanticipated, but welcome nevertheless, letter had arrived today of all days. A previous letter she'd received from France a fortnight or so ago was still occupying her mind as she thought of talking to Elodie about the possibility of going away for Christmas.

The arrival of that first letter had aroused an unexpected and deep desire in her to spend Christmas in her home town. This longing to visit Antibes Juan-les-Pins one more time hadn't gone away. Instead, it had grown roots and settled in. The arrival of this second letter today made it even more imperative that everything was in order for Elodie's sake. There was no way she could stand by and see her beloved granddaughter lose out on the inheritance she had planned to leave her. Talking to Elodie about both the past and the future would be far easier if they were in France. She'd be able to see and judge Elodie's reaction when she told her the truth about certain things she had never spoken of before.

The socca finished, her mind unexpectedly resolute, Gabriella stood up. It was time to return to France, to lay some ghosts. Now there was a genuine reason to return she just needed to persuade Elodie to accompany her to the south of France for Christmas without revealing the reason for their visit until they were there. A plan started to form in her mind. A simple plan but one she was sure Elodie would agree with. And once they were in France, she'd to talk to Elodie and tell her about certain secrets from the past.

She, Gabriella Jacques, was going to spend Christmas in Antibes Juan-les-Pins for the first time in forty years.

2

Elodie Jacques pushed back against the expensive ergonomic office chair she'd treated herself to for her twenty-fourth birthday two months ago and ran her hand through her hair as she looked despairingly at the words on the computer screen in front of her. There was only so much you could say about a, so called, revolutionary toothbrush that, in essence, looked the same as its predecessors. She didn't have the energy that afternoon to dream up a 'buy me and I'll change your life' type pitch that the company wanted for their Christmas advert. All she could think of was the Pam Ayres poem, 'I wish I'd looked after me teeth.' Which wouldn't do at all. At All.

This wasn't the life she'd dreamt of four years ago when she'd completed her media degree and decided to be a journalist. She'd be a journalist for a year or two while writing a novel in her spare time that would turn out to be a bestseller after which she'd switch into being a full-time novelist. But writing copy for an advertising company had somehow become her main income stream along with the occasional paying feature in the newspapers. Sitting in front of the computer and writing to order every day drained her creativity and she was no closer to writing her novel than she had been four years ago. Occasionally she managed to write a short coffee break story of 800 words for one of the women's magazines but fiction was a diminishing market in the days of 'Real Life' stories both in print and on line. Maybe she should write and sell her own recent real-life story, a fictitious account, of course, about how 'a friend' had escaped a controlling boyfriend. A tremble ran through her body. The fewer people who knew the truth about that relationship the better. She hadn't even told her grandmother, Gabby, all the details, and eight months down the line she still felt stupid and let down over the whole thing.

Elodie sighed. She knew she was lucky to live in the same home she'd grown up in with her grandmother, who was more of a surrogate mother really. Gabby had looked after Elodie since she was a three-year-old toddler and her mother had married and gone to live on the other side of the world, leaving her only daughter behind at the behest of her husband. Elodie had spent years wishing her mother would return but by the time she was ten she'd more or less accepted the fact that the woman who had given birth to her didn't want to be part of her day to day life.

When she was younger, Elodie had taken the role her grand-mother played in her life for granted. It was only as she grew older that she realised how hard it must have been for her grand-mother when her own daughter had taken off, leaving her with no option other than to look after the child she'd left behind. The hurt she must have felt deep down both for herself and the small child who called her Gabby, rather than grandma or granny. Communication didn't cease totally. There were letters a couple of times a year and always cards and presents at Christmas and for birthdays but never a single visit in the last twenty years.

Elodie had occasionally dallied with the idea of turning up

unexpectedly at her mother's last known address and demanding answers but had always decided against it on the grounds that it was down to her mother to put in an appearance in her life. She was the one who had left. Besides, who knew where she was these days. There was no address on the birthday card she sent recently. She could be anywhere in the world.

Elodie wasn't sure when she began to feel something akin to hate for this woman who professed to love her but whose physical presence was missing from her life. Her replies to the letters, her 'thank you's' for the presents, became shorter and shorter and had turned into an irksome duty by the time she was a teenager, prompting Gabby to take over the correspondence completely.

Elodie heard the front door slam downstairs. Her grandmother was back from town. Earlier she had offered to drive Gabby and her friend, Maud, to Torquay, the nearest large town, to do some Christmas shopping and to see the lights. Gabby had declined the offer, saying Maud was busy this afternoon, and she'd walk into Dartmouth and catch the bus back if she bought anything. Neither of them had lots of people to buy presents for. Her absent mother had told both of them very firmly in a letter, years ago, that she didn't want anything in exchange for the gift vouchers she sent every year, and it was easier for her to send vouchers as she didn't know what they liked or what they had. Which Elodie felt was mean of her but was relieved to be let off the hook of having to find a present for a stranger who had no part in her life.

As for friends, working freelance from home meant there weren't any office buddies to bond with or to chat to over coffee. Elodie knew she could count everyone she was remotely close to on the fingers of one hand and still have a spare finger: Gabby, Carole and Beth, her best friends from school, and Maud. She knew too, that Gabby had only a handful of close friends to buy presents for although she would make dozens of mince pies for the various Christmas coffee mornings held in town to raise money for charity.

Elodie quickly saved the page she'd been working on and closed down the computer. Maybe, after a cup of tea with Gabby, she'd be inspired with a catchy toothbrush phrase or two and she'd finish the piece this evening.

3

Gabby was placing a couple of mince pies from the batch she'd made that morning on a plate when Elodie walked into the kitchen.

'They look good. Is the town full of Christmassy atmosphere?' Elodie asked.

'Lights are good this year. But I'd forgotten the council had planned to have a French market,' Gabby said. 'Took me right back.'

'Was that a good thing or not?' Elodie looked at her grandmother who gave a shrug in response before turning away to make the tea.

Elodie knew better than to probe Gabby. She'd either talk to her or not but she wouldn't be surprised if seeing the market had upset her grandmother. Gabby couldn't help being unmistakably French in attitude and the way she dressed but anything connected to the country of her birth had been steadfastly ignored for as long as Elodie could remember. There had been the odd occasion when something or other had triggered a memory and Gabby had been quiet and withdrawn for an hour or two but soon recovered her equilibrium as she pushed the memory away again. What her life had been like before she left France all those years ago, Elodie had no idea. It was never talked about. Gabby had always kept her own counsel.

A few crumbs were all that was left of the mince pies before Gabby gave a deep sigh and looked at Elodie.

'You know I'm seventy at the end of this month? I'd quite like to celebrate my birthday this year.'

'Really? You've always insisted on just a card and a token present, no fuss. You've never let me organise a party or treat you to a meal in a nice restaurant for any of your birthdays,' Elodie said. 'But that's great. Dinner at the restaurant of your choice? Tell me which one and I'll book a table.' Elodie's fingers were crossed as she said that. Gabby's birthday was on December 31st and restaurants were invariably booked up months, even years, in advance with New Year party bookings.

'The Hôtel Belles Rives would be wonderful.'

Elodie gave Gabby a puzzled look. 'Don't know that one. Is it new? Where is it?'

'Antibes Juan-les-Pins.'

Elodie, stunned into silence for several seconds, looked at her grandmother.

'You want to celebrate your birthday in France?'

Gabby nodded slowly.

'Not only my birthday. I want you and me to spend Christmas and New Year in Antibes Juan-les-Pins.'

Open-mouthed and lost for words now, Elodie stared at Gabby.

'For goodness sake, close your mouth. Good job there aren't any flies around,' Gabby said.

'Why celebrate this year? And why in France?' Elodie managed to ask.

There was a short pause while Gabby fiddled with her cup and saucer before standing up and placing them in the sink and then returning and sitting down opposite Elodie.

'It was this afternoon at the French Market. I had a slice of socca and it was, oh so good, memories of growing up in Antibes Juan-les-Pins came flooding back. Happy memories that I've pushed away along with the bad ones, and I had this overwhelming feeling that I needed to go back to see it all again. To feel the warmth and the sun on my face. To show you around.' There, that was all true, she hadn't lied. Elodie would find out the real reason when they were there.

'It won't be the same place you left behind all those years ago,' Elodie said gently. 'It will have changed.'

'I realise that but I suspect the essence of the place will still be there despite the new roads and buildings that have been built in the last decade or two. Besides, the sky will be bluer and the sun shines down there far more than it does here and we both could really do with some sunshine.'

'The Riviera is a very popular destination these days, if we do decide to go, we may have a problem finding somewhere to stay.' Elodie said. 'How soon before Christmas did you want to go, and how long after New Year do you want to stay?'

'A few days before Christmas to give us time to settle, say the twentieth, and,' Gabby paused. 'Perhaps return on the third of January?'

'A fortnight then?'

Gabby nodded thoughtfully. 'That should be long enough.'

'Won't a stay of that length on the Riviera be expensive? Maybe just a week would be better?'

'A week isn't long enough,' Gabby said, a decisive edge to her voice. 'Besides, think of the money I've saved over the years by not returning – I can spend it all now on a once in a lifetime holiday, for us both.' She held up her hand as Elodie went to protest. 'It will be my treat, no arguments.'

'Okay we will talk about that later. I'll fetch my laptop and we'll see what we can book.' Elodie pushed back her chair and stood up.

Two hours later flights had been booked – outward on the twentieth of December and back on the third of January. Finding accommodation had been harder. Elodie had vetoed booking into a hotel on the grounds of expense, besides, being independent would give them more freedom, freedom to do what, she wasn't exactly sure. She spent ages searching for an Airbnb, eventually hitting the jackpot with a two bedroom apartment in a block just off the coastal road in Juan-les-Pins. Gabby had taken one look at the photograph of the sitting room in the modern block and declared it to be 'Parfait!', before heading for the kitchen and opening a bottle of her favourite red wine and pouring two glasses as the confirmation e-mail arrived.

Handing one glass to Elodie she raised the other in a toast. 'Here's to Christmas on the Riviera,' and the two of them clinked glasses before taking a sip. As she drank the red wine, Gabby mentally started to write the reply, now she knew what she was going to say, to the letter that had arrived that day. A reply that might or might not be acceptable. If it wasn't, well, there was a New Year coming and she resolved to try again in January.

Elodie, feeling shell shocked from the speed at which things had fallen into place from the moment Gabby had voiced her desire to go to France, shook her head. 'I still can't quite believe what we're doing.'

'Stop worrying. We're going to have a lovely Christmas and New Year – it's a long time since I've felt so excited. A Christmas adventure for us both,' and Gabby took a drink and smiled at Elodie over the rim of her glass.

Elodie looked at her grandmother. Was there more behind this unexpected desire to return to the town where she was born, after decades of practically denying its existence, than she was saying? And when did the holiday become an adventure?

4

TWELVE DAYS LATER.

The plane slowly lost height as it flew over the Mediterranean until it was lined up in exactly the correct position to land safely on the runway that bordered the sea at Nice airport. Elodie, tense in her window seat, looking at the lights twinkling along the coastline and watching the fast approaching sea, let her breath go as she felt the wheels hit the tarmac and the plane began to slowly taxi towards its arrival slot.

'That was exciting,' Gabby said. 'I remember that take-off is interesting too but we don't have to worry about that for a while yet.'

They followed the other passengers into the airport building and had their passports checked and stamped before carrying on to the baggage collection point. Once they'd lifted their luggage off the carousel conveyor belt they walked unhindered through the 'Nothing to Declare' customs door and seconds later were out in the crowded Arrivals Hall with its large Christmas tree, glitzy decorations everywhere and a make-believe Father Christmas, his sack over his back, apparently climbing one of the balconies.

Screams of delight and happy laughter filled the air as families were reunited.

As they walked onto the airport concourse Gabby said, 'Come on, let's find a taxi.' There was a short queue at the taxi rank but ten minutes later they were in a sleek Mercedes heading away from the airport.

It was late in the afternoon and the bord de mer was busy with traffic so the journey was slow but they were both more than happy to look out of the windows at the passing scenery. Elodie, with barely concealed delight, gazed at the Christmas lights and inhaled the atmosphere of the Riviera that she sensed in the air. She stared unashamedly at the luxury cars with their glamorous passengers idling at the traffic lights, impatient for the green to flash so they could be on their way. Scooters weaved in and out of the traffic, seemingly without a care in the world, making her fear for their safety. Even the pedestrians and dog walkers on the pavements had an air of glamour about them.

Gabby, meanwhile, was struggling to come to terms with the fact that she barely recognised anything she was seeing. She heaved a sigh of relief when a few minutes later the taxi came to a halt in a queue of traffic and she recognised the curved apartment blocks of the Baie des Anges. Villeneuve-Loubet. She'd seen the first of the four pyramid like buildings under construction before she'd left. At least she could now estimate how far from Antibes Juan-les-Pins they were. As the traffic lights changed to green, Gabby bit her bottom lip and stared resolutely ahead. Another fifteen or twenty minutes, depending on the traffic, and she would be back in the town where she was born. A town she'd loved and somewhere that circumstances beyond her control had forced her to leave. Was she making yet another mistake in her life by coming back at this late date? What if? Gabby shook herself. She mustn't think like that.

Rational thought told her that nobody would recognise her, that there was nothing to link the old woman she had become with the young woman she had been. And if they did, so what? Hadn't she decided that it didn't matter if they did? The world had moved on, was more accepting of things that had once carried great stigmas.

'You were right, Gabby,' Elodie said, breaking into her thoughts. 'We are going to have an adventure, not just a holiday. I'm so looking forward to you showing me around. Do you think anyone you went to school with will still be living here? Didn't you tell me once that you had a best friend called Colette when you were young? D'you remember her address from then? You could go and knock on her door.'

Gabby shook her head. 'No. Colette left France at the same time as me. She went to America.'

'Shame. But not all the people you grew up with will have left, we'll have to do some detective work and see if we can find one or two. Invite them for a drink on your birthday, even have a party.'

Gabby gave a non-committal, 'Mmm,' as the taxi pulled up outside a large apartment block, relieved that she didn't have to say anything that would encourage Elodie on that subject.

Gabby gave a sharp gasp as she got out of the taxi and stared at a large white building a few hundred metres further down the street. 'Why didn't I notice how close the apartment is to this building as we drove up? I know it's dark now but the street lights are on.'

'No idea,' Elodie said, wondering why her grandmother looked so shocked at seeing a building which, judging by the scaffolding along two sides of it, was undergoing major renovations. 'It looks to have been a wonderful building in its day, not that you can see much of it under the tarpaulins and scaffolding.'

As Gabby turned away to pay the taxi driver after he'd placed their suitcases on the pavement, a woman came out of the apartment block's main door.

'Madam and Mademoiselle Jacques? Welcome. I'm Jessica Vincent, owner of the apartment. Come on in and I'll take you up.'

Huddled together in the small lift carrying them up to the eighth floor, Jessica chatted away in a friendly manner, explaining that she and her French husband, Mickaël, lived in the penthouse apartment and they weren't to hesitate to go up if they needed help in any way. 'Your surname is very French but I'm thrilled you're actually from Devon, my home county. To be honest, you're our first guests. We were quite surprised to get a Christmas booking for this year, we'd only been registered on the site two hours before you booked it.'

'It was such a last minute thing for us, I was beginning to feel we'd never find anywhere. Finding your advert with a vacancy was like a miracle,' Elodie said.

Stepping out of the lift, Jessica walked a short way down the corridor before opening a door and ushering them into the apartment and switching on the lights.

'This is lovely,' Elodie said. 'Even nicer than it looked in the web photos.' Pale sunshine yellow walls, cream carpets, a three seater red leather Chesterfield settee and two matching armchairs.

'The apartment can sleep six if necessary, as the settee converts into a comfortable bed if you have any friends dropping by unexpectedly,' Jessica said. 'There's extra bedding in the cupboard if you need it.

'You overlook La Pinède from the rooms and the balcony on this side, there's even a glimpse of the sea. No sea view from the bedrooms I'm afraid,' Jessica said, opening one of the doors. 'Just a few villas and, of course, the old Hôtel Le Provençal at the bottom of the street.'

'We saw the scaffolding.' Gabby walked across to the bedroom window. 'What's happening to it?"

Jessica shrugged. 'We'd hoped that finally the latest plans to turn it into luxury apartments would actually happen but they were derailed again and it's been abandoned once more. Such a shame. I'd loved to have seen the place in its heyday.' Jessica joined Gabby at the window.

'So sad to think it's just been sitting there empty and deteriorating since 1976. My father-in-law tells me it was the in place for decades, anybody who was anybody stayed there.'

Gabby nodded. 'Indeed, they did.'

Jessica gave her a quick look. 'You knew it back then?'

Gabby gave a brief nod. 'I knew of its reputation for sure.' When she didn't say any more, Jessica turned away and Gabby followed her out of the sitting room into the kitchen where she pointed to a welcome basket on the work surface.

'A few things in there to keep you going for this evening.' Jessica said and pointed out the contents of a small dish next to the basket. 'Code for the main door, two keys for the apartment door and the wifi code. Right, I'll leave you to settle in,' and she walked to the door. 'I hope you enjoy your stay. Oh, I nearly forgot. Please come up and have a Christmas aperitif with us on the twenty-third, seven o'clock. See you then if not before.'

As Jessica left, Elodie began to inspect the contents of the welcome basket. Several cheeses, slices of ham, chicken and sausage, baguettes, red wine, coffee, milk, and a box of artisan chocolates.

'Mmm, it all looks delicious but shall we dump our cases in the bedrooms and go for a walk first?' Elodie looked at Gabby. 'I can't wait to explore. We can settle in and have supper when we get back.'

'Good idea,' Gabby said. 'I could do with stretching my legs and getting some fresh air after the flight.'

5

Five minutes later, Elodie slipped the apartment key into her pocket with the code for the foyer door and they went down in the lift. Once outside, they walked down towards the main road and crossed over before making for the centre of Juan-les-Pins. Gabby led Elodie past the park, Pinède Gould, where the stage for the annual Jazz Festival was erected, and on towards the maze of narrow streets leading to the sea front. The early evening air was cool, Christmas lights and decorations were sparkling and the pavement tables of bars and cafés lining the streets were full of happy laughing people enjoying the festive ambience. Elodie gave a happy sigh. 'It all feels so French. Silly, I know to say that but,' and she shrugged.

Gabby nodded absently as she looked around. Things were more built up than she remembered but the cafés were as busy as ever, the people as stylish, and the atmosphere around them as they walked couldn't, as Elodie had said, be anything but French. Her forty year absence melted away as they walked – and she, Gabriella Jaques, inwardly recognised and accepted the fact that this place was her true home.

'Was there a casino here when you were growing up?' Elodie asked as they walked past the steps of the entrance to one.

Gabby laughed. 'Juan is the place it is because of the casinos that brought the place alive in the roaring twenties. The one we've just passed was the original, I think.'

'Did you ever go? Play cards or roulette?'

'I worked in that one for a few months,' Gabby said. 'Not as a croupier, behind the scenes.' Time to start telling Elodie snippets from the past; prepare her for the surprises she intended to break over the next week.

'I never gambled there, employees weren't allowed in the gaming rooms. I actually left the casino to work at the Hôtel Le Provençal. Jessica was right when she said it was the place to stay. I enjoyed that much more and I met some famous people there.'

Elodie looked at her grandmother. 'You're a dark horse. Working in a casino and a luxury hotel – why have you never told me this before? Which famous people did you meet? Would I have heard of them?'

Gabby shrugged. 'Some. The Rolling Stones, Tom Jones, Ella Fitzgerald, oh, there so many but it was all such a long time ago a lot of them will have died. The casino wasn't much fun, to be honest, but the hotel, that did have its moments.' Those moments, although pushed deep into the recesses of her mind, she'd never forgotten.

'But in 1968, the year I started working at the hotel, there was a lot of unrest all over France, general strikes and riots in Paris and Bordeaux. The students in Cannes were particularly militant too and they managed to get the Film Festival closed.' She shook her head. 'Hard to imagine now.'

'Shame the hotel isn't still in business we could have celebrated your birthday in style there.'

Gabby shook her head. 'No. Not even if it was still open. Too many memories. Come on. I'll treat you to a glass of mulled wine from that pop-up stall over there.'

Sipping their mulled wine, they wandered along, stopping now and again to look at various Christmas displays and to window shop. As they placed their empty cups in a waste bin, Gabby looked at her watch. 'Shall we head back to the apartment? Have supper and settle in? We can explore more in the morning.'

Elodie's tummy rumbled as if in answer and she laughed. 'Definitely need something to eat now.'

'It will be quicker if we go down here,' Gabby said, pointing to a narrow street. 'We should come out near the apartment block if I've got my bearings right.'

Five minutes later they'd crossed the main road where fairy lights were wrapped around the trunks of the pine trees that gave the town its name and the apartment block was within sight. Walking past the abandoned Hôtel Le Provençal hidden behind tall shuttering Gabby felt her mood darken and she quickened her steps. She'd known, of course, when she'd suggested coming here for Christmas and New Year that some hard to cope with memories would be thrown up by returning. What she hadn't expected was to be staying so close to a building that would be a constant reminder of the life she'd left behind all those years ago.

An iconic building that had played such a large part in her life at the time and had been an inherent presence in deciding the direction of her life.

After supper, as they tidied the kitchen together, Elodie happily agreed with Gabby when she'd suggested an early night.

'Good idea, then we can be up early and make the most of our first day.'

'I had no idea travelling could be so tiring,' Gabby said, before giving Elodie a goodnight hug and disappearing to her room.

Elodie was thoughtful as she made her way into her own room and began to unpack her suitcase. She had a feeling there was more than pure tiredness behind Gabby's desire for an early night. Her grandmother had been animated and happy walking into town, wandering around and then walking back, until they'd reached the building site that was the Hôtel Le Provençal. It was as though something inside her had been instantly switched off at the sight of it. A memory too far maybe? But tonight was only their first night down here, there were sure to be more memories thrown up, how would Gabby cope for the next week or so?

Elodie sighed as she placed her clothes in drawers and hung things in the wardrobe. Maybe it had been a mistake to agree to this holiday. She should have realised it would be difficult for Gabby even though it had been her idea to come. But in truth, she had no knowledge of Gabby's early life, no idea whether it had been good, bad or indifferent. Or even happy as opposed to miserable. It wasn't a subject that had ever been discussed.

One thing Elodie did know though, was that her grandmother had always been there for her and she intended to return the support in any way it was needed. Gabby could never be rushed, she would open up about things when she was ready, which meant that Elodie would wait quietly until the time was right.

Zipping her now empty suitcase closed Elodie placed it in the bottom of the wardrobe and shut the door. Should she suggest to Gabby they cut their losses and return home if it was making her unhappy? Such a waste of money if they did leave and besides, now she was here, she personally, longed to explore the place, see for herself some of the famous French Riviera loved by so many. Deep in thought, she slipped her laptop out of its bag, placed it on the small table in front of the window and opened it up.

Determined to make the most of the unexpected holiday,

Elodie had written all her commissioned features before leaving home and was now looking forward to doing some writing of her own. While they were there, she planned to keep a daily diary, to do some research for a couple of travel articles she had in mind and start the novel she'd been dreaming about forever. Tonight's early bedtime was the perfect opportunity to make a start on the diary and maybe also start planning an outline for her novel.

6

Following a restless dream filled night Gabby was up early and quietly made her way to the kitchen to make a cup of coffee. Back in her room, sitting in the cane chair by the window sipping her drink, she tried to assess her feelings about returning to her home town. And particularly her reaction to being so close to her old workplace, the Hôtel Le Provençal. It was only a building, she told herself, an inanimate construction that over at least four decades of the twentieth century had been witness to the dazzling lifestyles of the glamorous with their self-indulgent demands and love of luxury. At one time, being able to say one was staying at Hôtel Le Provençal with its Art Deco decor and celebrity guests was to tell the world that you had made it. Even working there had had a certain prestige about it, as if the glamour rubbed off onto the hotel staff by some form of osmosis.

When Gabby joined the staff in the late 1960s, she'd recognised that the hotel had taken on the mantle of a beloved dowager and whilst not exactly threadbare it was definitely in need of some TLC. It was still loved by its guests though, many of whom came to try and catch a glimpse of its former glory and see the elaborate chandeliers and Art Deco decorations that were left. Gabby smiled to herself, remembering how thrilled she'd been to be employed as a trainee receptionist. From the day she started she'd loved the job and the feeling of being an important part of a successful team responsible for the smooth running and reputation of the hotel. By the time she was a fully fledged receptionist she not only took the faded opulence of her daily surroundings for granted, she'd stopped being over-awed by the stars who were regular guests throughout the year, and others who flocked to the place in May for the Cannes Film Festival. Most of the guests were gracious and polite to the staff although there were, of course, exceptions. Then Gabby smiled and carried on doing her job with a steely reserve. Her secret ambition in those long ago days was to be Head Concierge but realising that was unlikely to happen because that important position was still regarded as being firmly in the male domain, she'd aimed instead for Head Receptionist. A position that was within her grasp when everything in her life went wrong.

Was that why seeing the hotel unexpectedly when they'd arrived had shaken her so much? The fact that it had taken her thoughts straight back to a time when life had been so full of promise only to have it snatched away? She shook her head. She'd blame the mulled wine for dulling her senses and making her emotions rise to the surface yesterday evening as they walked back. She'd be on her guard to stay in control of those emotions today while they were out and about.

Gabby finished her now cold coffee and, glancing at her watch, stood up. Seven thirty and still dark. She'd have a shower and then go in search of the boulangerie for breakfast croissants. Half an hour later she let herself out of the apartment and set off. If the boulangerie she remembered with fondness was no longer there at least the bakery in the supermarché on the seafront would be open by now. She walked along the bord de mer making for the maze of small streets that ran parallel to it, hoping that it or at least a successor, was still in business. The smell of warm bread in the air pulled her along and after a right turn into a side street, she happily joined the queue of housewives and small children waiting to buy their daily breakfast croissants and their coffee break treat of macaroons. Gabby smiled to herself. The boulangerie might have acquired a modern make-over but the enthusiasm of the French for their daily croissants and cakes remained unchanged.

By the time she returned to the apartment the sun had risen in a pale blue sky promising a fine day and the roads and pavements were busy. When Gabby opened the apartment door Elodie had the coffee machine set up and was writing a shopping list on her phone.

'Breakfast,' Gabby said, waving the paper bag. 'It's warm enough to sit out on the balcony. Bring the coffee and we'll sit and watch the world go by while we make plans.'

'You were up and about early,' Elodie said. 'Couldn't you sleep?'

'Bit restless, to be honest. Now, what are we doing today?'

'I'd love you to show me around, point out the places of historical interest like where you were born, where you went to school, etcetera, back in the dark ages.' Elodie laughed at the look on her grandmother's face. 'Only if you want to, of course,' she added, remembering Gabby's reaction to seeing the hotel last night. 'But I do want to explore and we need to do a food shop, maybe have lunch somewhere, wander around the Christmas market and decide how we are going to celebrate Christmas.'

'Let's forget me showing you the sights of historical interest today and concentrate on organising ourselves for the next few days' Gabby said. 'There will be time enough between Christmas and the New Year to do that.'

They left the apartment an hour later having decided to get the food shopping out of the way to leave the rest of the day free. In the supermarket Elodie was captivated by the amount of oysters, mussels and langoustines piled up near the fish counter, boxes and boxes of them. Thoughtfully, Gabby stood looking at the lobsters available from the large tank at the back of the fish counter.

'This takes me back. Christmas Eve is the big celebration with family here and the main meal is always sea food. Since I left, I've always done things the English way and celebrated Christmas with a special roast meal on the day.'

'Do you want to do it the French way this year? You know I'm not that keen on oysters and mussels,' Elodie said. 'But if you want a fish meal on Christmas Eve we could get some prawns? Have a salad with them?'

Gabby shook her head. 'No, I'm not that keen on seafood either.' She turned and began to push the trolley away from the fish counter. 'We should decide though, if we are eating in or out over the holiday. I suspect we will have left it too late to book a table for Christmas Eve but we could possibly find somewhere for lunch on the twenty-fifth but it's doubtful that it will be a roast dinner.'

'I think I'd like to eat both meals at the apartment – sitting out on the balcony if the sun is shining and it's warm enough,' Elodie said. 'Shall we decide on menus later and come back for a festive food shop tomorrow?'

'Good idea.' And the two of them concentrated on finding the basics like coffee, teabags, butter, salad stuff, potatoes, yoghurts, bread, some cooked meats, cheese and wine – rosé and red.

Once they'd returned to the apartment, unpacked and put the

food away, they headed back out into town and rewarded themselves with a coffee and an éclair at a café on the front overlooking the sea.

Sitting there under a blue sky with the sun shining, Elodie sipped her coffee before looking at Gabby.

'Are those pharmacy signs with the temperature always right? There's one over there showing seventeen degrees.'

'They're usually accurate,' Gabby said. 'And that temperature is about what I remember for a December day. Gets colder in January and February, usually and it's not unknown for there to be snowstorms down here.'

'Do you ever wish you'd never left here? I mean if nothing else, the weather is better,' Elodie laughed.

Gabby was quiet for a moment, thinking of the letter in her bag. The truthful answer would be, 'all the time', but she couldn't risk saying that to Elodie because it would invite the questions, why did she leave then, followed quickly by, why didn't you come back if you regretted it? The answers to those two simple questions were no easier to answer than they had ever been. While she did plan on telling Elodie the truth sometime during the holiday perhaps it would be better to get Christmas out of the way before delving in and bringing up the past. Who knew what the consequences of that might be.

'In some ways I wish I'd never left but the opportunity to return never happened.' The words, until it was too late, remained unspoken. 'Besides, life goes on like it does. No point in dwelling on lost opportunities.' Gabby pushed her empty cup away and stood up.

'Come on, there are lots of little artisan shops in the back streets. Let's go and see if any of the ones I remember still exist. We know the boulangerie does.'

As they wandered around Gabby chatted to Elodie about

inconsequential things related to growing up in the town in the fifties and sixties. Nothing to invite meaningful questions.

'I remember the highlight of summer in the sixties being the Jazz Festival. Everything was always so much fun then. Or maybe it was because I was a teenager lucky enough to be alive during the 'Swinging Sixties. Although they do say if you can remember them, you weren't there.'

'And do you remember them?' Elodie glanced at her grandmother curiously.

'Mostly.' Gabby said, smiling at her with a twinkle in her eyes. 'Although there are one or two small gaps, which I have no intention of discussing with you.'

'Spoilsport.' Elodie stopped in front of an estate agents' window. 'There's some lovely properties down here. Can you imagine living in that wonderful Belle Époque villa,' she said, pointing to a photograph and sighing. 'I'd love to look around it. But the price. D'you think we could blag our way into a viewing?'

Gabby shook her head. 'No chance. All viewers of properties like that are usually vetted very carefully and by that I mean they have to prove they have the means to purchase before they can put a foot over the threshold.'

'Shame.'

'Look, there's the mini shuttle bus, shall we jump on and head into Antibes itself? We could walk along the coast but it's quite a way.' Gabby said. 'There's sure to be a big Christmas market there in one of the squares. We can do the coastal walk another day at our leisure.'

Twenty minutes later and they were standing on the Esplanade du Pré des Pêcheurs down by the harbour looking at the Christmas market which had been set up there. There were traditional wooden chalets selling an amazing variety of goods, an accordion player wandering around playing a mixture of carols and popular songs and delicious smells drifting on the air from various food stalls. The ice skating rink was busy with young children whizzing around while their anxious parents urged them to be careful from the edge of the rink. Christmas fun was definitely in the air.

'Where to begin?' Gabby said, ever practical. 'We have to have a plan, we don't want to miss anything.'

'How about we go clockwise, starting from here with the outside row and get closer to the middle stalls in ever decreasing circles?' Elodie suggested. 'Would that work?'

'Let's find out,' Gabby said and they set off.

Time disappeared as they wandered from stall to stall. Some stalls claimed Elodie's attention more than Gabby's, and vice versa, and the other one would wander on and then they'd reunite a few stalls later. Gabby was standing in the queue by the socca stand when Elodie joined her, having dragged herself away from an artisanal stationary stall where she'd been drooling over a selection of notebooks and pens.

'I'll go and get a couple of coffees, shall I?' Elodie asked. 'Or there's sure to be the ubiquitous mulled wine stand if you want?'

'Coffee will be fine,' Gabby said.

Ten minutes later, sitting on a bench on the outskirts of the market, they ate and drank what constituted their missed lunch, whilst watching the scene in the market.

'How can something so simple taste so good?' Elodie smothered a sigh as she finished her slice of socca and Gabby glanced at her.

'Something the matter?'

'No, I was just thinking about other people's Christmases, how busy they are. All these families out and about, skating, present buying, food buying, celebrating with family and friends. Whereas we,' Elodie shrugged. 'Well, it's always been you and me, which is fine,' she added hastily. 'I'm not complaining, just wondering what it must be like to be part of a larger family. What was Christmas like when you lived here?'

'Neither of my parents had any siblings, so there weren't any aunts, uncles or cousins around for me either,' Gabby said. 'Christmas was a special time for us but it wasn't the huge commercial affair back in the fifties and sixties that it is these days. I always got a book and a new dress for Christmas, one that was kept for Sunday best throughout the next year.' She smiled at the memory. 'By the time I left school and started earning my own money things had moved on.' Gabby gave Elodie a concerned glance.

'Is that what you dream about? Having your own family?'

Elodie nodded. 'I can't help wondering whether it's ever going to happen, to be honest. Carole's getting married next year and Beth has a new boyfriend whom she thinks is The One. Of course I'm happy for them both but worry that I'm being left behind.'

Gabby, lost in her own thoughts about a certain letter, was silent for a moment or two. 'All I can say is life has a funny habit of sorting things out at the right time. It might throw a couple of curve balls in your direction but in the end they can turn out to be the very thing you need, although it's impossible to see that at the time. You're only twenty-four and I know it's a cliché but you never know what's around the corner. You'll meet someone special one day and hopefully create your own family, maybe have three or four children, and then you'll remember our quiet Christmases with nostalgia.'

Elodie looked at her grandmother. 'I'll remember them always with love and gratitude, not just nostalgia.' As they stood up Elodie enveloped her grandmother in an unexpected hug. 'Right now, I've got all the family I need. You.'

7

After their improvised lunch the two of them had a final wander around the remaining stalls and Elodie managed to sneakily buy a small but beautiful ornamental white owl as a novelty present for Gabby. Equally sneakily, Gabby bought a journal and a pen for Elodie from the stationary stall and hid them in the bottom of her bag.

As the evening drew in they walked slowly up through the town marvelling at the street decorations as the lights came on and dusk fell. 'That is so beautiful,' Elodie said, looking up at the gossamer effect of strings of chandelier like lights that were looped and draped down the length of several of the streets. There were decorated Christmas trees everywhere – on the streets, in shop windows and in the windows of apartments above the shops. A mini fun fair for children on Place Nationale was swarming with families and the food market they discovered on Place de Gaulle had both Gabby and Elodie buying festive treats.

Elodie found a box of delicious looking artisan chocolates sprinkled with gold that she said were perfect to take to Jessica's on the twenty-third. 'Can't go empty handed for aperitifs.' And

Gabby bought a wicker basket filled with a selection of nuts, nougat, mini Calissons d'aix en Provence and some jellied fruit.

'Some of the thirteen desserts we need,' she said. 'We can get the bûche de noel and the Pompe à l'huille tomorrow.'

Elodie looked at her. 'Thirteen desserts, really?'

'When in France, yes.' Gabby smiled. 'I'll explain the tradition to you on Christmas Eve.'

Elodie spied a DIY shop down a side street with artificial Christmas trees on sale. 'That's what we need in the apartment,' she said and virtually ran into the shop. Ten minutes later she re-appeared, clutching two long boxes and carrying a bag containing three sets of fairy lights and with a big smile on her face.

'Any chance of a bus or a taxi back to Juan?' she said. 'I think I got a bit carried away.'

Fifteen minutes later, after finding a taxi and being driven through the inland streets the taxi stopped outside the apartment block. Gabby punched the entry code into the outer door and they entered the building as Jessica and Mickaël, her husband, stepped out of the lift. Jessica introduced Mickaël before apologising and saying they had to dash because they were meeting their son at Nice airport. 'See you both on the twenty-third,' she called out as Mickaël ushered her through the open door.

Once up in the apartment, Gabby offered to organise supper while Elodie sorted out the Christmas trees and lights. By the time supper was on the table, there was a tree standing in front of one of the windows, throwing back the reflection of the long string of white lights Elodie had wrapped around its branches. A string of coloured fairy lights were draped across the curtain rails and Elodie was putting the finishing touches to the second tree in front of the other window.

'There,' she said standing back and surveying her handiwork.

'It's not Christmas without a few fairy lights. We need to buy a couple of candles tomorrow too.'

Over supper they discussed the festive food shop they were going to do in the morning and Elodie entered the shopping list on her phone. After supper, Gabby switched on the television in the corner of the room and flicked through the channels before they finally settled down to watch a film on Netflix. As the film credits rolled Gabby switched the television off and stood up.

'I'm going for a stroll before bed – fancy joining me?'

Elodie hesitated, torn between wanting to go and write in her diary and not wanting her grandmother to go wandering late at night on her own.

'Just a short one,' Gabby said sensing her hesitation. 'I thought I'd go a little way along the coast road away from town towards the Port Gallice Marina.'

Crossing the road before they reached the high scaffolding and hoarding surrounding the Hôtel Le Provençal they made their way towards the marina. Walking past the entrance of the Hôtel Belles Rives with its flags hanging on either side of the doorway, they heard the sound of revelry inside. Elodie turned to Gabby.

'Isn't this the hotel where you said you wanted to celebrate your birthday?'

'Yes, not that I really meant it,' Gabby said. 'It was just the name I came up with when you asked about my birthday.'

Elodie smiled. 'It looks like a good place for a celebration.'

They walked on until they reached the road entrance to the marina where, by mutual consent, they turned and crossed the road and began to make their way back.

As they walked they both stared up at the upper floors of the old hotel that had dominated the skyline for decades. The shuttering, fencing off the Hôtel Le Provençal site from inquisitive pedestrians with tall hoarding, ran along the length of the pavement and frustrated Gabby. She slowed her pace as they walked past the site, stopping occasionally to try and peer through non existent gaps. At the very end there was a small space where it joined the hoarding from the side and Gabby stopped and strained to get a glimpse of what was going on. A long ago memory forced its way to the surface and flooded her mind.

Growing up in Juan-les-Pins she'd heard all the stories, the legends about the Hôtel Le Provençal. The famous stars like Josephine Baker, Mistenguett and Ella Fitzgerald who had all given impromptu performances there. Important people like John F. Kennedy, Winston Churchill, Coco Chanel and the Duke of Westminster had all stayed there at various times. Welshman Tom Jones had made his international debut in the night club there. While the marble steps and stairways were still intact and chandeliers still hung in the public rooms, the art deco decor and fittings were showing their age but somehow the very walls of the hotel conveyed the glamour of past times. When she got the position of trainee receptionist she was beyond thrilled to be working in such a famous place.

Elodie's anxious voice broke into her thoughts. 'Gabby, are you okay? Shall we get back?'

Gabby took a deep breath and smiled at Elodie. 'Sorry, I was just remembering. Yes, let's get back.' And she began to walk briskly up the road without telling a curious Elodie about her thoughts.

Once back indoors, Gabby gave Elodie a quick goodnight hug. 'I'm off to bed.'

'Are you all right?' Elodie asked. 'You seem a bit withdrawn.'

'I have a couple of things on my mind,' Gabby said. 'And I'm probably still a bit tired from the journey and today has been a busy one. A good night's sleep and I'll be fine. I'll see you in the morning,' and she opened her bedroom door.

But Elodie wasn't letting her go that easily. 'You would tell me if there was something wrong? Or something bothering you?'

Gabby nodded. 'Of course I would. I promise we'll talk soon.' And the bedroom door closed behind her.

Elodie bit her bottom lip as she went to her own bedroom. Well, that was interesting. One moment Gabby was denying anything was wrong, in the next she was saying they would talk soon. A contradiction almost in the same breath. And deny it all she wanted, Elodie knew that Gabby hadn't been herself this evening, especially since that little episode outside the old hotel. Had it brought back upsetting memories for some reason?

In her own room, Gabby took the two letters that had prompted this journey out of her bag. The handwritten one she put down on the dressing table, whilst she re-read the business like typed one before refolding it and placing it back in her bag. Tomorrow she'd walk into the centre of Juan-les-Pins and make a rendez-vous for a day in the week between Christmas and New Year. She picked up the handwritten one and, standing in front of the window, she re-read it. The two letters had both arrived completely out of the blue – a piece of pure serendipity – bringing two curve balls back into her life, forcing her to take action and face the past. Carefully she refolded the letter and placed it back in her bag. One day soon she would show it to Elodie.

In the meantime, she would try to and find the right moment to talk to her granddaughter about the other important issue she needed to deal with during the holiday.

8

As they ate their breakfast croissants the next morning Gabby glanced at Elodie. 'Fancy seeing one of those sights of historical interest, as you put it, this morning?'

'Yes please,' Elodie said. 'Which one?'

'The house I was born in.'

Half-an-hour later, after walking along the front before turning into the back streets of Juan-les-Pins, Gabby stopped at the entrance of a tucked away impasse.

'Here we are.' The cul-de-sac in front of them had the feeling of being in the countryside with its tall eucalyptus tree in the middle of a roundabout like a village green. There were several well spaced early twentieth century villas surrounding it. Not quite Belle Époque in style but still beautiful in Elodie's eyes.

'This is lovely. It feels special,' Elodie said, looking around and counting the villas as they walked slowly down the road. 'Which one did you live in? Whichever, it must have been wonderful growing up in any of these houses.'

'Yes, it was. We lived in No.5,' and Gabby pointed to the villa they were approaching at the head of the cul-de-sac.

The eight villas around the green were all Provençal in design with the requisite red roofs, olive green shutters and Juliette balconies on the second-floor rooms. Set back from the road, large electric gates at the individual entrances protected their privacy. Elodie was disappointed to see the large pair of white electronic gates at No.5 were, like all the others, closed, and the tall hedges bordering the sides of the entrance and enclosing the garden made it impossible to see more than the upper storey and the red tiled roof. She'd been hoping to, at least, get a view of the front of the house.

Gabby, at her side, was silent and deep in thought, her eyes taking in changes only she could see as her mind recalled how it was years ago.

'Were the villas as shut off from each other as this when you were growing up?' Elodie asked.

Gabby shook her head. 'No. Everyone knew everyone and they were friendly. No electric gates in those days but it is different now. People want to feel safe from intruders and keep themselves to themselves.'

Gabby fell silent, the memories of earlier, happier times flooding into her mind and sweeping away other thoughts.

'Such a shame we can't see more of the house,' Elodie sighed. 'Do you ever wonder who lives in it now?'

Gabby took a deep breath. Time to start telling Elodie the truth. 'I know who lived there until recently. A couple with teenage children. They had a boutique in Antibes, I believe. But their business closed and they've moved away.'

Elodie turned and stared at her. 'How on earth do you know that?'

Five, ten seconds passed. Gabby sighed. 'Because they rented the house from me,' she said quietly. 'Come on, I've got the keys, we can have a look around.'

A stunned Elodie fell into step alongside her grandmother as she made for the gates of the villa, pulling a bunch of keys from her bag. Elodie watched her in silence, her mind reeling with questions as Gabby found the remote hanging amongst them and pressed it. How long had her grandmother owned the house? Why had she never told her before? Why had she chosen to come to France this particular year?

The gate swung open easily and they stepped into the garden surrounding No.5. Gabby with apprehension and Elodie with excitement. As the gate clanged shut behind them they both looked at the villa standing at the head of the short drive in front of them. Elodie with a smile of delight and Gabby struggling to hold back her tears.

The front door, a sturdy oak one, was in the middle of the building, a short flight of four shallow steps leading up to it. Olive green shutters were closed over the windows on either side of the door. Underneath the windows were granite troughs filled with spring bulbs, daffodils and tulips, already breaking through the soil.

'It's lovely,' Elodie said. 'It's like all the pictures of houses in the south of France I've ever seen. All that's missing is the requisite rampant bougainvillea smothering one of the walls.'

'There's one on the back wall – there always used to be anyway. Maybe it's died or been cut down by now,' Gabby said, climbing the steps and reaching up to a lock at the top of the door where she inserted a key and turned it, before bending down and pushing a different key into another lock and finally turning the door knob.

'That is a serious number of locks,' Elodie said, looking on in surprise.

'There was a spate of burglaries a few years ago along the coast and the agent told me they were necessary for the tenant's peace of mind.' Gabby opened the door and Elodie followed her in. Gabby automatically reached for the light switch that had always been on the left-hand side and light flooded into a wide hallway with a terracotta tiled floor.

Two doors faced each other halfway down the hall and Elodie hesitated. 'Kitchen on the left, room on the right used to be a spare room,' Gabby said. 'Probably empty at the moment. Yes, it is,' this as she opened the door and looked in.

Elodie opened the kitchen door and peered in as Gabby once again found and pressed the light switch. White units down one wall and a farmhouse table in the centre with five chairs around it. 'Lovely size,' Elodie said, turning back to the hall.

Further down the right-hand side of the hallway, and before the curved arch at the end of the hall opened into a large empty room, a flight of wooden stairs led to the first floor. At the far end of the large room there were three sets of double French doors, currently all tightly shuttered. Doors on the left-hand side of the room opened onto a shower room and toilet and a utility room.

'This is a big house, Gabby,' Elodie said, shaking her head in disbelief. 'Were your parents wealthy?'

'My father's family were, they owned a lot of property in the area. My father inherited everything, including this house. Sadly, he was not a businessman and in the end this place was virtually all he had left.'

Gabby unlocked one of the French doors, lifted the bar on the shutter and pushed it open. Stepping out into the garden, Elodie took in a large swimming pool, a pool house and a summer kitchen over to one side of the garden with a barbeque and pizza oven. Tucked around the side was a shed which contained cane furniture and neatly stacked gardening tools.

Elodie, about to ask Gabby how she could have ever given up life, not only in Juan-les-Pins, but also here in this beautiful house, suddenly realised how quiet she had gone and gave her a hug.

'It must be difficult for you being back here after so long?'

Gabby nodded.

'Shall we lock up and leave?'

'Please.'

Quarter of an hour later, Gabby had secured the shutters again and locked the front door. Once they were back outside on the pavement Elodie made sure the electric gates were closed and they made their way out of the cul-de-sac. Elodie had so many questions she wanted to ask but the visit had clearly distressed Gabby and Elodie didn't want to make things worse. She was sure Gabby would talk to her when she was ready.

To her surprise, they'd gone about twenty metres when Gabby took a deep breath and began to speak about the past without any prompting.

'I need to tell you some things. My mother died twenty-three years ago, not long after you were born and my father about ten years ago. After his death I inherited the villa, whether I wanted it or not.'

'Why wouldn't you want it? It's a lovely house.'

Gabby glanced across at her. 'My father disowned me when I was about your age and cut me out of his life. French law, though, dictated that as his only child, he couldn't disinherit me. I know he wouldn't have left it to me if he could have avoided it.'

A shocked Elodie wanted to ask 'why did he disown you?' but intuition told her that it was the wrong time to ask Gabby that particular question.

'Did you ever think about coming back and living in the villa?' She asked instead.

'It briefly crossed my mind when I was told it was mine but

you were fifteen, important exams were coming up, it just didn't seem the right time to uproot you.'

'You could have discussed it with me.'

'Yes, I should have done that.'

'Why didn't you sell it?'

'I did think about it but decided the best thing would be to treat it as an investment for the future for a couple of years, until you'd finished college, at least. I intended to tell you about it then, see if you'd like us to move to France but you were happily settled into your job, and I... I guess I just let things drift.'

Gabby walked in silence for a few moments. 'Letting things drift is proving to be a blessing in disguise though. Property on the Riviera appears to hold its value in a similar way to that in Paris and the house is worth a lot more now than when I originally inherited it. And, although some of the rent money has been used for general maintenance over the years, most of it is in a savings account in your name. I have to tell you there is a large amount of money there now.'

Elodie stopped and stared at her grandmother. 'Seriously? I've got a nest egg savings account with thousands in it? Like some trust fund kid.'

Gabby nodded. 'Yes. Next year, when you're twenty-five, you'll have full access to it.'

Elodie, trying to get her head around the fact that on her next birthday she would apparently inherit a large sum of money, ran her hand through her hair. It was going to take some getting used to. She turned to Gabby.

'Are you thinking of selling the villa now?'

Gabby's tone was flat as she answered. 'Somebody has been in touch with the agency that manages it for me, asking if it's for sale. It would be a good time to let it go now it's empty.'

'Is seeing the house again before putting it up for sale the real reason you wanted to come here after all this time?' Elodie demanded.

'One of the reasons. Another reason was me wanting to lay a few ghosts. Get closure over certain things, is the way I think you youngsters would put it.' Gabby shook her head when Elodie gave her a curious look. 'Another time. You need to think about the house, help me decide what is the right thing to do. Rent it out again or sell.'

Elodie smothered a sigh. She could tell her grandmother was struggling with her emotions at that moment and she slipped her arm through Gabby's.

'There, now you know about the house I can relax a bit.' Gabby exhaled a breath. 'Come on, I think we both could do with a glass of mulled wine from that pop-up stand on the front.' And she lengthened her stride as if she couldn't get away from the area fast enough.

9

The rest of that day and the next passed in a whirl of Christmassy food shopping and turning the apartment into a home from home for the next ten days or so. Festive food shopping was divided between the artisan delicatessen they discovered in one of the busier streets off the sea front, the boulangerie for bread and a decadent chocolate and cream bûche de noel and the rest, including a couple of bottles of champagne, they bought in the supermarket.

Candles, books and magazines were purchased and placed on the small table in the sitting room. Elodie couldn't resist treating herself to a cream throw with popular images of France scattered over it for the settee. 'For my bed at home. I can squash it into my suitcase when we leave,' she said to Gabby. 'A lovely reminder of our holiday.' A popular music channel was found on the television and the fairy lights and candles helped transform the functional rented rooms to a more personal, happy and cosy space.

Both Elodie and Gabby ventured out separately, Elodie with a street map open on her phone and Gabby with the memories of the streets of her childhood still embedded in her mind. Elodie discovered the Tourist Office whilst meandering around Juan-les-Pins on the second afternoon and picked up lots of tourist brochures, including one for a Belle Époque villa close by on the Cap d'Antibes. She was disappointed to discover that it only opened its doors to the public from April to October.

'We'll have to have a return trip,' she said to Gabby when she got back to the apartment. 'Now you've brought me here I want to come again and again. It's wonderful. I'd love to have a holiday here in the summer.'

'Summer is hot and full of tourists. Spring or Autumn would be better,' Gabby said. 'I'm off out for a walk but I'll be back in plenty of time to get ready for drinks at Jessica's tonight.'

'Okay. I'm going to do some work on my laptop,' Elodie said.

Walking slowly through the town, Gabby reflected on how the place had changed. The unchanging layout and narrowness of the streets and the older buildings lining them spoke of its history but the face that it presented to the world these days was a modern twenty-first century one. So many apartment blocks lining the bord de mer. So much traffic. So many cranes towering over everything and building yet more apartment blocks. But somehow it still called to her in the way, in secret, it always had. And now Elodie had fallen in love with the place. Was that going to be a good thing? Or would it cause problems?

Gabby sighed as she pushed open the glass door of a double fronted shop and walked in. A young woman wearing a red Santa hat smiled in welcome. 'Bonjour Madam.'

'Bonjour. I'd like a rendez-vous as soon as possible after Christmas with Monsieur Albrecht, s'il vous plait.'

The woman pulled a desk diary towards her and turned the page. 'Would ten thirty suit you on Monday, the twenty-eighth?'

'Perfect. Thank you.'

'Name?

'Madame Jacques.'

'Oh.' The girl looked at her. 'Monsieur Albrecht has been waiting to hear from you. He is free at the moment if—'

Gabby shook her head. 'No. I have other things to sort out first. Monday will be fine. Merci.' She gave the woman a smile and left.

Making her way back to the apartment, Gabby felt a surge of relief. All she had to do now was to talk to Elodie over the next few days and prepare her for what was likely to happen in the next week. Hopefully, by the time of her rendez-vous with Monsieur Albrecht she would have an inkling, at least, of how things were panning out.

Whilst Gabby was out, Elodie opened her laptop and tried hard to concentrate but found it impossible. Her attention kept drifting off to thinking about No.5. After telling her about the house yesterday and saying 'There, now you know about the house,' Gabby hadn't mentioned it since. But something in the way Gabby had spoken as she'd looked at her, made Elodie think she was still holding something back. And she couldn't help wondering why her unknown great-grandfather had disinherited his only daughter.

Elodie sighed. Gabby was her only blood relative – there was very little point in counting her absentee mother who had relinquished the role – and she loved Gabby more than she could say. Now though, she was uneasily aware of how little she knew about her grandmother's past life. Why had she been disowned by her family? Surely she regretted leaving Juan-les-Pin? It was hard to imagine Gabby as a young woman, working in a casino and later at the Hôtel Le Provençal. That was another thing, Gabby had seemed strangely distressed by the proximity and the state of the old hôtel, and Elodie couldn't help but wonder why.

Restlessly she picked up the tourist brochures she'd collected.

So much to see and do down here. Maybe next week, after Christmas, she could persuade Gabby to take a day trip to Cannes, another to Monaco. A boat trip to St Tropez was out of the question this time but would definitely be on the list for the next visit. Another visit to see inside No.5 again would be good too. Because it wasn't just a case of either renting it out again or selling, there was a third option that hadn't seemed to occur to her grandmother, but it was certainly buzzing around in her own mind.

In the meantime, she'd start to write down ideas and thoughts before she forgot them for a 'Spending Christmas in Antibes Juan-les-Pins' feature she hoped one of the glossy magazines would be interested in next year. Then she'd do a bit more work on the outline of her novel. Feeling more optimistic and determined she pulled her laptop towards her and began to work.

Two hours later, there was a gentle tap on the bedroom door before Gabby poked her head around.

'Elodie, love, you need to get ready. We're due upstairs in about thirty minutes.'

'I totally lost track of time,' Elodie said, saving the document on her laptop and closing it down. 'Don't worry, I promise I'll be ready in time.' Like her grandmother, she too, hated being late for anything. Twenty-five minutes later, she'd showered, applied the minimal amount of makeup she always wore, slipped on the nearest thing to party wear she'd brought with her, a favourite red dress, and joined Gabby in the kitchen.

Gabby pushed a plate of bread and butter towards her. 'I know there will be finger food with the drinks but a slice or two of this first won't go amiss.'

'Thanks.' Elodie said, picking up a piece and nibbling it. 'How many people do you think will be there?'

Gabby shrugged. 'No idea. Are you worried about it?'

'A bit. You know how dodgy my French is despite your coaching.'

'You'll be fine. Having to use it will be good for you,' Gabby said. 'Come on. Time to go. Don't forget the chocolates.'

10

The lift was already in use going down so they elected to climb the two flights of stairs to the penthouse, rather than wait for it to return. The door to the penthouse was open and they hesitated on the threshold taking in the large Christmas tree, the background music and the loud hub of people already in a party mood. As they stood there trying to see either Jessica or Mickaël, Jessica saw them and rushed over to welcome them.

'I'm so glad you came. I was afraid you wouldn't, I know how terrifying the prospect of facing a room full of strangers can be,' she said, leaning in towards them and speaking quietly. 'But none of these will bite, I promise.'

'We brought you these as a thank you,' Elodie said handing her their gift.

'Thank you, that's kind of you. Now, let me get you a drink and then I'll introduce you to a few people.'

Elodie's heart sank as she realised introducing them to people involved separating them. Mickaël came over and took Gabby away to meet 'the old reprobate that is my father' and Jessica insisted she had to meet their son, who was spending Christmas and New Year with them.

'Several of his friends are here tonight. Much better for you to spend time with them than us old fogeys.' Jessica looked around the crowded sitting room before finally spying her son chatting to people on the balcony on three sides of the penthouse. 'There he is. Come on.'

'Oh, please leave him with his friends, I don't want to be a nuisance,' Elodie said, knowing from the look Jessica gave her she was wasting her breath. She smothered a sigh and followed Jessica out onto the balcony, wondering which of the four men in the group would turn out to be her son. Turned out to be the sexy intellectual looking one wearing the heavy framed tortoiseshell glasses.

'Elodie, this is my son Gaspard, unfortunately known as Gazz because he won't answer to anything else. Gazz, this is Elodie who's staying in the Airbnb with her grandmother. Be nice to her and introduce her to your friends.'

'Sure thing, maman,' Gazz said, before turning to Elodie and smiling. 'Enchanté,' and he held out his hand for her to shake before starting to introduce her to the others. 'Anatole and Emilie, Cal, Denis, Fiona and Carla.' As he finished the introductions, Fiona moved to his side and placed a possessive hand on his arm while smiling sweetly at Elodie. Elodie smiled sweetly back but she got the message she guessed she was intended to loud and clear and turned to answer Carla who asked where she was from.

'Devon, on the south coast of England. Where are you all from? Antibes, or have you moved here from different parts?'

'Fiona and Cal are interlopers from Nice, the rest of us grew up together,' Gazz said easily. 'We know each other's every secret, don't we, guys?'

The banter between the seven of them was light-hearted.

Elodie listened to them with a smile even though she was unable to contribute much to the conversation as it was spoken in rapid fire French. Eventually she tuned out for a few moments. Glancing back into the sitting room she saw Gabby next to a man she presumed to be Mickaël's reprobate father and laughing at something he'd said. Elodie couldn't remember a time when she'd ever seen such an animated look on Gabby's face. She was clearly enjoying herself and Elodie was glad.

Gazz soon realised she was struggling to understand them and started to quietly translate things for her. Then the others, apart from Fiona, made a point of speaking to her in a mix of French and English and as she relaxed, she managed to answer a couple of times in French. She learnt that Gazz lived in Paris and that he did something important in banking, that Cal and Emilie worked in IT up in Sophia Antipolis, Fiona and Carla worked as legal secretaries and Denis and Anatole were both vets.

'We need refills and maybe some food,' Gazz declared and the group moved back into the crowded sitting room.

Elodie looked across to where Gabby had been sitting but there were a couple of strangers there now and no sign of her grandmother or Mickaël's father. She wouldn't have left without letting Elodie know so had probably simply moved somewhere quieter. In an apartment this big there was sure to be a quiet room somewhere.

The group of friends had been separated as they moved through the crowd towards the table where the drinks and plates of nibbles had been laid out for people to help themselves. Gazz was at her side and he was repeatedly stopped and Elodie found herself being introduced to several people, whose names she was ashamed to realise, she immediately forgot. Eventually though, the two of them reached the buffet table and Elodie reached for some olives and a couple of blinis spread with pâte. Gazz glanced at his watch.

'Think I'll skip eating here. Would you like to join me and the gang for supper in Juan?' Gazz said, as he topped up her glass of champagne.

Elodie shook her head, remembering Fiona's possessive hand on his arm. 'You don't see your friends very often. I wouldn't want to intrude. Thank you for the invite but no.'

They were joined at that moment by Fiona and the possessive hand was once again placed on his arm.

'Gazz darling, the others are ready to leave, shall we find your maman and say our goodbyes?'

'You and the others go ahead, I'll catch you up in about five minutes. I need to check on something first.'

'I can wait,' Fiona said.

'No point. I'll see you at the restaurant.' And he gave her a quick kiss on the cheek, leaving Fiona with no option but to turn and go. Elodie recoiled from the glare she received as Fiona walked away. She glanced at Gazz, wondering if he realised he'd just breathed out a quiet frustrated sigh.

'If people are starting to leave, I'd better find Gabby,' Elodie said. 'Aperitif invitations are usually for about an hour, aren't they? The time has gone quickly thanks to you and your friends. It's been lovely meeting you all.' With one exception, she thought, but didn't voice.

'You are here until January and so am I, so I'm sure we'll see each other again,' Gazz said.

'That would be lovely. Gabby was with your grandfather earlier but they both seem to have disappeared,' Elodie said, looking around.

'In that case I think I know exactly where she'll be. Follow me.'

* * *

Gabby had hidden her irritation at being almost frogmarched to meet Mickaël's father simply, she suspected, because they were the same age group. But there was something about the man who reached for a silver topped cane and struggled to his feet from the couch he'd been sitting on as his son introduced them. Something she couldn't quite put her finger on, other than he reminded her of Jean-Paul Belmondo, the French actor she'd been a fan of. Perhaps it was just that.

'Please, don't get up,' Gabby said automatically speaking French as Mickaël introduced her. Philippe looked at her.

'I have always stood up for a lady, and I always will, but now I sit again.' And he gestured to her to sit alongside him before sending Mickaël off to fetch them a bottle of champagne and a platter of nibbles. Mickaël duly did as he was told. Placing them on the table in front of the couch he winked at Gabby. 'Have fun.'

Philippe poured them both a glass of champagne and they clinked glasses. 'Here's to new friends,' Philippe said. 'I suspect we are going to be good together.'

Gabby looked at him and smiled. 'Anybody ever called you out for being impulsive? We might hate each other.'

Philippe shook his head. 'Hate is such a waste of emotion. The opposite is so much better and one should grasp every opportunity for the possibility of that.'

Gabby, knowing full well what the opposite of hate was, shook her head at him. 'No wonder your son called you a reprobate. You're incorrigible.'

'But I'm also fun and at our time of life we need fun otherwise it's all so bloody depressing.'

Knowing she couldn't argue with that Gabby laughed and changed tack.

'Why the stick?'

'New hip a month ago. Another few weeks and I'll be able to whirl you around the dance floor.'

'Nice thought but I'm afraid not. I'll be back in England by then.'

'I didn't say where the dance floor would be. Besides,' Philippe paused. 'Now you are here, will you find it easy to leave again, Gabriella Jacques?'

'How...?' Gabby's voice trailed away as she stared at him.

Philippe shrugged. 'I put the two and two together and made five,' he said. 'You speak French like a native and your surname isn't English. How long have you been away?'

'Too long. There were difficulties to my returning before.' Gabby gave him a wry smile. 'But I'm beginning to think I made them bigger obstacles than they truly were. Anyway, I'm here now, ready to sort certain things out.'

'Anything I can help with?'

Gabby looked at him. Some instinct told her that his offer was a genuine one, that he was a man she could trust. She shook her head. 'No, not really but it would be good to talk things through with someone. Get a different viewpoint. See if I'm doing, have done, the right thing. If you're willing to listen and advise?'

Philippe struggled to his feet. 'Pick up the champagne and follow me, leave the nibbles. If we're going to talk about the past we need some privacy.'

Surprised, Gabby did as he instructed, and, aware that people were watching their progress with interest, followed him out of the sitting room, down a short corridor and into a book lined room with a large desk and a couple of easy chairs. The biggest computer screen Gabby had ever seen stood on the desk.

'My study. Nobody ever comes in here but me,' Philippe said, standing by one of the chairs and gesturing to her to sit before carefully lowering himself into the other one.

'You live here with your son and daughter-in-law?'

'Yes. But the apartment is big enough to have been divided into two so we can escape from each other. I have my own rooms including a bathroom and kitchen. It works well. Most of the time.'

'Why the huge computer?'

'Why not? Big is good. I watch a lot of sport on it.' Philippe said. 'Now please top up our glasses and tell me all.'

Gabby poured the champagne and handed Philippe his glass, not quite sure where to begin, or even how much to tell him. It was a long time since she'd had anybody to confide in. He waited patiently while she gathered herself together and began to speak, instinctively playing for time to put her thoughts in order.

'We're obviously quite close in age but you weren't here when I was growing up, were you?'

'No, I was born along the coast in Frejus. My father moved the family here in the early seventies. I've lived here ever since.'

'I left in the early seventies.'

'We could have met years ago. Shame, all those wasted years when we could have been friends,' Philippe said with a sigh.

'Did you ever go to the Hôtel Le Provençal before it closed?'

'Once or twice but it was past its best and I was young. There were newer, sexier places opening up all around.'

'I worked there. I thought I'd met the love of my life there,' Gabby said quietly. 'Sadly, I wasn't his.'

'Employee or guest of the hotel?'

'Head Receptionist who became Concierge.'

There was a five second silence before Philippe spoke, his words gentle. 'Would that be Christophe Lampeter by any chance?'

Gabby closed her eyes as he said the name and nodded. 'You know him?'

'Yes.'

Gabby waited for him to say more but he shook his head and waved his hand at her. 'Another time. Continue.' She took a deep breath.

'Elodie, my granddaughter thinks spending Christmas here in France was a last minute decision of mine. But it wasn't. Something I received gave me the idea a couple of weeks before I suggested it to Elodie. And now I'm scared that trying to do the right thing, even if it is years late, will make even more problems. At my age you'd think I'd know better than to meddle.'

Philippe reached out and took her hand. 'One never knows how another person will react. Doing things from the heart for the right reasons always turn out for the best in the end but sometimes, yes, it does cause more difficulties along the way. Gabriella, do you mind if I call you that? It's such a beautiful name for a beautiful woman, much better than Gabby.' He smiled and said 'Bien' as she nodded her agreement.

'Whatever it is you've set in motion, will be.' He stopped and let her hand go as the door opened and Gazz and Elodie appeared.

'Thought we'd find you here, Papa Philly. Hello, Elodie's grandmother, I'm Gazz.'

'Hello Gazz, lovely to meet you,' Gabby said, shaking his hand in a daze as she wondered what Philippe had been about to say.

'People are starting to leave so I thought it was time for us to do the same,' Elodie said looking curiously from her grandmother to Philippe and back again.

'Yes. Of course.' Gabby moved towards Philippe who had struggled to his feet and was now standing leaning on his cane.

'Thank you. It was – interesting – meeting you. Happy Christmas.' She smiled at him and went to turn away but Philippe caught hold of her hand and gently pulling her forward whispered something only she could hear. She blinked hard at his words and forced herself to move. Were the words he'd whispered 'Do not forget we are now comrades in arms' the words he'd been about to say when they were interrupted?

'Come on, Elodie we must find our hostess and say our thank yous.' Gabby walked out of the study with a bemused Elodie and Gazz following her.

Gazz took the lift down to their floor with them and wished them both a cheery goodbye. 'Enjoy the rest of the evening. À bientôt.' And the lift gates closed behind them and he disappeared.

'He seems a nice young man,' Gabby said. 'I look forward to seeing him again.'

'Mm,' Elodie agreed, thinking about the possessive Fiona. 'You and Philippe seemed to be getting on well.'

'Yes, he's a real gentleman despite Mickaël calling him a reprobate, although I think he probably was back in the day.' Gabby smiled.

After they'd both changed into their everyday clothes they worked together in the kitchen preparing the ham and cheese toasties they'd decided on for supper. Once they were under the grill Elodie went through to the sitting room, switched on all the fairy lights and lit a couple of candles. She stood for a few moments, looking at the lights of Juan-les-Pins spread out in front of her and the lights of the traffic moving along the bord de mer.

Wishing she'd been brave enough to accept the invitation, she briefly wondered which restaurant Gazz and his friends were in, what they were eating, and how serious was Gazz's relationship with Fiona. The last thought brought her up short. Why was she thinking about that? She'd only just met Gazz, it was none of her business whether he was in a serious relationship or not but she couldn't help wishing that he was single and the two of them could be friends.

Elodie sighed. It wasn't as if he'd been flirting with her, he'd just looked after her, making her feel special, as if she mattered to him. You're reading too much into his behaviour, she chided herself. It's probably just the way he is.

'À table,' Gabby said carrying their supper into the room. Elodie turned away from the window and joined her grandmother at the table, trying to push all thoughts of Gazz Vincent out of her mind. In much the same way that Gabby, sitting opposite her, was determined not to think about her new friend, Philippe.

'A Merry Christmas to us all, my dears. God bless us,'

— CHARLES DICKENS. CHRISTMAS CAROL

11

————

Gabby woke early on Christmas Eve morning but didn't get up immediately, her conversation with Philippe still on her mind. She wished she'd had more time to talk to him, explain about the house and ask his advice, amongst other things. Seen his reaction and received his reassurance she was doing the right thing. Not that his reassurance was guaranteed of course, he might be horrified and be too polite to show it. No, she didn't know him well, but she suspected he would always be honest and tell her his true thoughts.

It was eight o'clock when Gabby finally threw the covers back and made for the power shower in the ensuite. Afterwards, as she dressed, she decided against coffee before she walked to the boulangerie, which was sure to be extra busy today before the shops closed for what was traditionally a half day. Taking her coat from the stand in the hallway, Gabby saw a folded piece of paper had been pushed under the door. Gabriella was scrawled across it in beautiful italic writing. She guessed even before she saw the signature at the bottom of the note it was from Philippe.

*Please have lunch with me today. I'll be down in the foyer
waiting for you at 12.30.*

   Philippe.

Her first thought was of Elodie. Would she mind being left
alone today? It was Christmas Eve but they hadn't made any
plans for Christmas other than to have a special meal tonight and
tomorrow and just generally 'chill out' as Elodie had put it. Gabby
put the note in her pocket and resolved to ask her over breakfast
if she minded. If the answer was yes, she'd go up to the penthouse
and make her excuses.

'Of course I don't mind you going out for lunch,' Elodie said
instantly when Gabby showed her the note as they ate breakfast.
'You've obviously made an impression there.'

'Don't be silly – it's just because we're both ancient and can
reminisce about the good old days,' Gabby said.

'Of course it is.' Elodie smiled at her. 'Fancy a walk and a hot
chocolate by the sea this morning, seeing as how it is Christmas?'

The promenade was busy and they were lucky to find seats on
the terrace of their favourite café. Sitting by the café's highly
decorated Christmas tree with its flashing lights, enjoying their
drinks as the French version of Jingle Bells playing on a loop,
floated out of speakers on the wall above their heads, Elodie
shook her head with amusement.

'Jingle Bells playing in the background, Christmas decorations are everywhere, but the sky is blue, the sun is shining and
there are even people swimming. Have to admit I'm finding it
hard to get my head around the fact that it is actually Christmas
Eve. So different to England.'

Gabby laughed. 'I have to admit I prefer this version of
Christmas Eve.' She looked at Elodie. 'When we've finished our
drinks can we walk back via the Provençal?'

'Yes, but why?'

'I noticed a gap in the hoarding the last time and I'd like to try and get a closer look at the place but I'd rather not go alone even though the place is deserted.'

Elodie shrugged. 'Okay.' She drained her mug and stood up. 'Come on then.'

Gabby led the way back to where she had seen the gap and showed it to Elodie. 'We can squeeze through here.'

Elodie glanced around to make sure no one was watching them. 'Go on, in you go,' and she watched Gabby squeeze through before she followed her.

'At least, technically it's not breaking and entering but I suspect we're trespassing,' Elodie said, joining Gabby as she stood looking at the building.

A building that was something and was now nothing. The white walls were flaky and discoloured, the state of the elegant front entrance of the hotel with its curved portico and elaborate columns was pitiful to see.

'Love the entrance,' Elodie said. 'Must have been very imposing in its day.'

Gabby nodded. 'It was. Not that I ever went in that way, it was the staff entrance down the side for me.'

The staff entrance all employees had to use, hidden out of sight around the side of the building. Every day she'd wrestle with the stiff latch of a substantial wooden door behind which a short flight of shallow steps led down to the basement where everything needed behind the scenes to run a luxury hotel was hidden. The kitchens, the large walk-in cold room, the laundry, the valeting services, the bed linen, the crockery. buckets and mops for washing the acres of uncarpeted floors, vacuum cleaners for the rest, trolleys for taking clean bed linen and towels to the 290 bedrooms, all this was placed as close as possible to one of the service lifts. Lifts the clients never saw or travelled in. The large staff room where employees could rest between shifts and eat their meals was adjacent to these service rooms.

The clocking on and off machine, ready to record everyone's start and finish times, was fixed to the wall close to the entrance steps. Impossible to miss. Several rows of lockers were also lined up in this space.

The people who worked in this 'below stairs' hotel community knew their place in the hierarchy of things much as the hotel's clients did. Of course, as the new trainee receptionist Gabby had quickly learned her own place was deemed to be above the cleaners but some-what below the bell boys until she was fully trained.

Gabby shook her head, clearing her thoughts. How much had changed since those days. She stood at Elodie's side, looking up at evidence that renovation work had started and then stopped. Modern guttering was in place, crumbling plaster had been chipped away and fresh applied and several windows had been replaced along the length of the top floor. New things themselves that were already showing a lack of maintenance.

Gabby shook her head. For the first time in decades she was standing in front of the building she'd adored and not liking what she was seeing.

'So sad to see it in this state,' she said. All the lower walls were covered in graffiti and Gabby prayed that all the wonderful Art Deco styling and decor she remembered inside the hotel had been rescued before the vandals struck.

Slowly she moved towards the portico. A large notice stuck on the main boarded up entrance told her in no uncertain terms 'Chantier Interdit. Keep Out.' Elodie followed her and tried to peer in through a ground floor window where the boarding had been hacked off by someone trying to break in.

'It's impossible to see anything,' she said. 'It's going to need someone with deep pockets to renovate a place this large. Probably better off demolishing it and starting again.'

'So much of its history has been lost already, to lose the building as well would be criminal. Jessica did say they were still hoping for someone new to step in and save it,' Gabby said. 'I've seen enough,' and she turned away.

They both squeezed back out through the gap and walked silently back to the apartment. Gabby with a heavy heart and Elodie feeling sad and unsettled for her grandmother.

'Can I ask you a question about what you told me yesterday?' she asked quietly.

Gabby looked at her and waited.

'You said your father disowned you but you didn't say why.'

'Because I was pregnant.'

Elodie looked at her, shocked. 'With my mother?'

'No. I was married to your grandfather when she was born,' Gabby's voice cracked. 'I lost that first baby but my father never forgave me. Called me a 'pute' amongst other things. But he was wrong. I was never a whore, I never slept around.' She turned anxiously to Elodie, wanting to explain. 'I was in what I thought was a serious relationship.' She shook her head. 'Times were so different back then.'

'He sounds a horrible unforgiving man,' Elodie said. 'I'm so sorry you went through all that and a miscarriage as well.' She put her arm through Gabby's before the two of them walked arm in arm back to the apartment in silence.

12

_____

When Gabby came out of her room ready to go down and meet Philippe, Elodie was sitting on the settee, her laptop on her knees.

'You will make yourself some lunch won't you,' Gabby asked.

'Of course I will. Although actually, I might go for a walk and buy a filled baguette and find somewhere to sit and do some people watching. Off you go. Enjoy your lunch.'

Philippe was waiting in the foyer for Gabby as she stepped out of the lift and greeted her with a kiss on both cheeks. Gabby glanced at him.

'No stick?'

Philippe shook his head. 'Non. It gives me the perfect excuse to take your arm,' and he proceeded to do just that. As they stepped outside a taxi drew up.

'Perfect timing,' Philippe said. 'We're only going about five hundred metres but I didn't want to risk over doing it,' and he let go of her arm to gallantly open the car door for her before walking slowly around and getting in the other side.

The short distance was covered quickly and the taxi dropped them outside a small bistro in a nearby side street.

'No sea view but the food is good,' Philippe said, 'and it's comfortable. I try to have lunch here at least once a week. They know what I like to eat and make me welcome without any fuss.' Something which was evident from the way he was greeted by the patron, who led them through the restaurant to a table with a reserved notice.

Once they'd both decided to go with the special Christmas menu du jour and its main course of Coquilles Saint Jacques, Philippe ordered a bottle of dry white wine, while Gabby looked around. The decor was unpretentious with simple wooden tables covered with pale blue linen cloths and comfortable cane chairs but the walls were something else. Every available space was covered with framed signed photos of famous people, mainly actors and singers but there were writers and a few politicians in the mix. From where she was sitting Gabby could see black and white photos of Picasso, Piaf, Hemingway, Josephine Baker, Maurice Chevalier, Mistinguett, Chanel, all huddled together on the wall alongside where they were sitting. She turned to Philippe.

'Some of these photographs were taken in the Provençal weren't they? I recognise the background.' Gabby longed to stand up and explore the other walls but the restaurant was too busy and she knew it would disturb the other diners. The waiter arrived at that moment with their wine and poured them both a glass before placing the bottle in a wine cooler.

She picked up her wine glass as Philippe held his out to gently clink hers. 'I thought you'd like it here. Before we leave there is one particular photo I want to show you.'

Gabby looked at him questioningly but he shook his head. 'Later.'

The meal was as good as Philippe had promised it would be and time disappeared as they ate, talked and laughed together while getting to know each other. Gabby looked at Philippe as she took a sip of her wine when the waiter came to clear their plates. It was years since she'd felt as relaxed and comfortable in a man's company as she did with him. Philippe, she suspected, had always had the effortless ability to charm any woman he wanted to but she was beginning to believe he genuinely did like her. She hoped so anyway, because it was a long time since she'd had a man as a close friend.

'What did you do before you retired?' she asked.

'I was a chef,' Philippe said. 'Not just a chef. A two star Michelin chef for a long time.' He shook his head. 'Sadly, the third star always evaded me but,' he shrugged. 'Two was better than most of my contemporaries. I even had a regular spot on television.'

'I've just realised who you are. You're The Philippe Vincent,' Gabby said pointing her finger at him. 'You were famous even in England. And you didn't swear in the kitchen like they all seem to these days.'

Philippe nodded. 'I am. They were good days.'

'You wrote a couple of cook books too. I gave my husband the barbeque one because he always took took charge of it and I was fed up with everything being charred to a cinder.'

'You have a husband?'

'No, not for a long time,' Gabby said. 'Much to the distress of my daughter who went off the rails a bit after he died.' She glanced at him.

'Your wife? I vaguely remember reading something about a tragic accident when you were at the height of your career?'

A sad look passed across Philippe's face as he nodded. 'It was a long time ago but sometimes it feels like yesterday.' Philippe twirled the wine in his glass around thoughtfully, before taking a drink.

Gabby sensed the sadness he was striving to play down and decided to change the conversation.

'I twisted Elodie's arm to come trespassing with me this morning. I wanted to take a close look at the Provençal,' she sighed. 'I wish in some ways I hadn't. So sad to see the state it's in.'

A couple on their way out greeted Philippe as they passed their table and wished him a 'Joyeux Noel.'

Philippe returned their greeting with a smile and waited until they had left the restaurant before standing up and holding out his hand to Gabby. 'Just time before our desserts arrive to show you the photo I mentioned earlier.' And he led Gabby across to the table where the couple had been sitting. The photos that covered the wall behind that particular table were again black and white with the exception of a coloured one on the far side. Gabby leant forward giving the photo of two men, arms around each other's shoulders, an intense stare for ten seconds or so. She recognised both men. One was a famous gay movie star back in the day whose name had deserted her as she looked at his companion and both signatures sprawled across the photo were illegible. Not that she needed to read them to identify the other man. She knew exactly who he was. And what the photo told her.

Gabby turned and Philippe held her hand as they made their way back to their table where their desserts were waiting. Sinking down onto her chair, Gabby shook her head.

'I had no idea. It all begins to make sense now,' she said, picking up her glass and drinking. 'At the time I thought Christophe just liked to play the field. He was never short of women chasing him. It never occurred to me he could be gay. I was so naive.' She took a deep breath. 'It's taken almost fifty years but least I know the truth now. It was him not me.'

Gabby picked up her spoon and began to break into the circular dessert of choux pastry filled with praline cream known as the Paris-Brest. 'My favourite dessert,' she said brightly. Philippe looked at her before reaching for her hand across the table.

'Gabriella, you are okay? I wasn't sure from the way you spoke yesterday evening whether you knew the truth about Christophe. I thought showing you,' he inclined his head in the direction of the photograph, 'would be the easiest way of telling you. I can tell it was something of a shock to you.'

'I'm fine, honestly. It was all such a long time ago and is best left forgotten in the past. And quite honestly, I have something more urgent to worry about at the moment.'

'My offer to help is always there,' Philippe said quietly. 'Comrades in arms, remember?'

Gabby regarded him thoughtfully and decided to tell him the truth, or at least some of it. 'I inherited a house here in Juan-les-Pins several years ago. The house I grew up in. It's been rented out for years and the rent money has largely gone into a trust fund for Elodie. I told Elodie about it yesterday for the first time and took her to see it. She loved it. Recently I was asked if I wanted to sell it and the answer is, I'm not sure.'

'Is the would be buyer pushing you to sell?'

'The agent is. I've got a rendez-vous with him after Christmas to tell him my decision.'

'So, a few days yet. If you were a gambler you could toss a coin – heads you keep or tails you sell. I think your hesitation is hiding what you truly want to happen. Gabriella, ma cherie, I think you already know what you want to do,' Philippe said.

Gabby closed her eyes and nodded. Philippe had seen into her soul. Seen what she hadn't admitted, not even to herself. She wanted to return and live in the villa.

'It wasn't practical, years ago, to move back and live here and it's no more practical now,' Gabby said. 'It's not just me to consider. It's Elodie as well. She has a job, friends, maybe not that many friends, but she's happy and settled.'

'She doesn't have to come,' Philippe said gently. 'You have a house in Devon, she could continue living there. Besides you could both simply divide your time between Juan and the UK at first. Have you asked her? Maybe she'd love to come and live in the south of France just like you want to.'

Gabby sighed. 'There's another problem now with that scenario that I haven't told you.'

Philippe looked at her. 'Tell me now?'

'You haven't asked me why my granddaughter, whom I've brought up since she was three, lives with me. It's because my daughter married a man who didn't want her child from a previous relationship and she chose to leave to be with him. Neither Elodie or I have seen her for twenty years. But the thing is,' Gabby stopped and looked at Philippe. 'I haven't told Elodie yet that her mother is unexpectedly back in England for good.' Gabby took a deep breath.

'I haven't mentioned either, that she's been in contact and that there is even a remote possibility she may turn up to join us while we are down here. And to be honest, I'm not sure how Elodie will react if that happens.'

13

After Gabby left to meet Philippe, Elodie closed down her laptop, grabbed her jacket and purse and walked down to the front. She bought a cheese salad sandwich, and a large coffee from the take-away catering van parked near the Pinède Gould and decided to sit on one of the nearby benches to eat it. It was quieter here and she wouldn't be distracted so easily while she thought things through.

She found an empty bench on the edge of the park and decided it would be the perfect place to eat. She unwrapped her sandwich and took a couple of bites, wondering as she did so how Gabby was getting on with Philippe and where he'd taken her. Elodie had never known her grandmother have lunch or dinner with a man before. But there was a lot she didn't know about her grandmother, she decided. Owning a villa down here and never mentioning it, for starters. She could understand Gabby not wanting to uproot her until she'd finished college but surely, after that, she could have, at least, told her about the place. And now she wanted her to help in deciding whether to sell it or continue letting it out without considering the third and more attractive option. Both of them moving to France and living in the villa. So many things would be better.

One, the villa was bigger than the house at home, they'd both have more room, and it would be lovely to have a pool. Two, the sky was bluer and the sun shone a lot more here. Three, it would get her out of the deep rut her life had sunk into. She'd just decided she'd suggest that option to Gabby tonight over their meal when Gazz sat down beside her, making her jump.

'Found you.'

'You have,' she agreed.

'Maman told me that my granddad was out with your grandmother which meant that you were alone. So, I thought I'd find you and see if you'd like to have lunch with me?'

Elodie held out the sandwich wrapper. 'I've just eaten.'

Gazz shook his head. 'That's not lunch. I'm talking about buying you the best pizza you've ever tasted. Come on,' and he grabbed her hand, hauling her to her feet. 'We need to get there before they stop serving.'

A minute later she was standing beside a Vespa scooter and Gazz was fiddling with the strap of the helmet he'd placed on her head, making sure it was secure.

'Umm Gazz, I've never ridden pillion on a scooter before,' she said quietly. 'And all the scooters I've seen down here are driven crazily.'

'You'll be fine. Just put your arms around my waist and hold on. I promise I'm a safe driver and won't go fast. Well, not too fast, anyway,' he grinned at her. 'There, comfortable?' She nodded.

He put his own helmet on, sat on the scooter and started the motor. 'Right, hop on. Arms round my waist, hold on tight and try to enjoy the ride.'

Elodie did as she was told and held her breath as they started to move. Soon she realised she was starting to enjoy the ride and that they were going away from Juan-les-Pins and heading for the back country. Twenty minutes later they arrived at a small town and Gazz came to a stop in a tree lined car park. They took off their helmets and walked up to the exit, down some steps and over the road.

'Welcome to Valbonne, one of my favourite medieval villages,' Gazz said.

'It's beautiful,' Elodie said, looking around at the ancient buildings. More than one Christmas tree stood in the main square and there were decorations and lights everywhere.

'Let's eat, then we can take our time wandering around afterwards.'

'I'd enjoy that. Maybe I can take some photos for a feature I can already visualise writing about this place,' Elodie said.

'I warn you, it's a favourite topic with lots of journalists,' Gazz said.

There were a couple of tables free at the main café and she happily followed Gazz as he made for one.

A waiter appeared handing them menus and took their drinks order, non-alcoholic beer for Gazz and a glass of red wine for Elodie. They were sipping their drinks and Elodie was looking around taking in the atmosphere when Gazz looked at her.

'You didn't say the other evening what you do but I'm guessing from your earlier remark that you're a journalist?'

'That's what I trained to be but currently I mainly write copy for adverts, the occasional feature for a glossy and the even more occasional short story for a magazine. Nothing remotely exciting. In fact, I feel my life is in a rut that is getting deeper by the day. I need to break out in the New Year.'

'I know that feeling.' Gazz said, nodding in sympathy. 'Which is why I've given my notice in at work, much to the horror of my parents, and I'm coming back here to live and work. Granddad Philly is on my side which helps.'

'What are you going to do?'

Gazz gave her a big grin. 'I've bought a windsurfing, sailing and jet ski hire business. Maybe you've seen the jetty on the front in Juan? End of January and I'll be operating my own business from there.'

'Sounds brilliant. Good luck with it. I expect Fiona will be happy to have her boyfriend living back down here.' Elodie said, jealously pushing away thoughts of Gazz ever being her boyfriend.

Gazz shrugged. 'Probably. But I think she, like my parents, would prefer me to stay in what they all consider to be a proper job.'

The waiter arrived at that moment with two large delicious looking pizzas and they both tucked in.

'This is so good,' Elodie said a few minutes later. Gazz grinned at her. 'Told you.'

It wasn't until they both replaced their cutlery on empty plates that Gazz looked straight at her. 'So, what are you going to do to get out of your rut?'

'Well, yesterday I discovered Gabby owns the house in Juan where she was born. My mission for the rest of this holiday is to try and persuade her to sell up in Devon and come here to live in it with me keeping her company, of course. All I really need is a good internet connection. I can be a freelance journalist anywhere. Might even be inspired to get that novel written. Think it's a plan?'

'Sounds good to me,' Gazz said. 'Come on. I'll settle the bill and give you a quick tour before we head home.'

Wandering around with Gazz as a quiet Valbonne prepared for the Christmas Eve festivities, Elodie felt an uplift in her feelings regarding the future. She was definitely going to talk to Gabby about moving down here because really, what was there to stop them?

14

Gabby was quiet as Philippe escorted her back to the apartment.

'Thank you for a lovely lunch,' she said as the lift stopped on her floor. 'And for being such a good listener.' She paused. 'Would you like to join Elodie and me for Christmas dinner tomorrow? You'd be more than welcome.'

'Lovely idea but I think you and Elodie need to talk, and Mickaël and Jessica expect me to join them,' Philippe said before leaning in and kissing her cheek. 'Joyeux Noel and I'll see you soon.'

'Joyeux Noel to you too,' Gabby said.

There was no sign of Elodie as Gabby let herself into the apartment and walked through to her bedroom. Standing out on the small balcony, the sun warm on her face, Gabby stared down at the Hôtel Le Provençal as the sunshine highlighted its decayed facade. She'd never imagined, all those years ago, it would end up in such a state, although, when she'd left she'd known that renovation was already long overdue.

The big American stars who liked everything to be in tip top condition much preferred to stay in the Eden Roc further down the Cap d'An-

tibes where their every whim was easily catered for in the opulent surroundings they favoured. Privacy and security were more guaranteed too. Although when the Cannes Film Festival was running several minor stars booked in and raved about what it must have been like in the past when Frank J Gould was in charge. Christophe had had a bit of a thing about the Goulds and their extravagant life style. Of course, he'd never met Frank, who died in 1956, or his wife, Florence, who sold the hotel then but he'd read everything he could get hold of about them. Gabby remembered Christophe had had a thing too, about the vintage fashions of those pre-war times and the early fifties. At work, he was obliged to wear the hotel uniform but off duty he stood out in his lounge suits, navy fedora hat and two-tone shoes. Gabby smiled to herself. Whenever they'd gone out together, it had always been Christophe people looked at, rarely her. She remembered having supper one evening in one of the cafés in town to celebrate his promotion to Deputy Concierge. They were with a group of their friends – well Christophe's friends, really – when one of them had smirked about his 'co-respondent' shoes. Christophe, who was very fond of his black and white leather shoes had become very irritated and gone off in a huff. The next day, she'd asked one of the older women who worked in the hotel basement about co-respondent shoes. 'They're flashy and the type of shoes a co-respondent to a divorce petition would have worn' she'd told Gabby with a laugh. 'As well as a certain type of man,' she'd added, 'if you get my meaning.' Which Gabby hadn't at the time but didn't want to admit to. She knew now though, after seeing the photographs in the restaurant and wished she'd been as streetwise in the old days as she was now. She could have saved herself a lot of heartache and broken off their relationship there and then. She wondered if Philippe knew anything about where Christophe was these days. If he was even still alive. The next time she saw Philippe she'd ask him if he knew.

Gabby went back out into the sitting room, picked up one of the magazines on the table and tried to concentrate on it but her thoughts kept jumping back and forth from the house to thinking about her daughter. Philippe had been right, moving to France and living in No.5 might be on the top of her wish list but so many things needed to be sorted before it could even be considered. Would Elodie come with her? Or would she prefer to stay in the UK? Would learning that her mother was back in the country make a difference one way or the other?

Gabby sighed. She'd had such high hopes when her daughter had made contact, hoping the breach between them would finally be healed and they could all move forward as a family but sadly it didn't look like it was going to happen anytime soon.

It was late afternoon before Elodie returned, with flushed cheeks and a smile on her face.

'D'you know the village of Valbonne?' she asked as she took a bottle from the fridge and poured herself a glass of water. Gabby nodded.

'Yes. But I guess it's changed a bit these days.'

'Probably, but it's still lovely. Gazz took me there on his scooter. We had a pizza in the main square. And then he showed me around. Did you know it's a fortified village based on a plan the monks on some island out in the Med created?'

'That would be St Honorat, one of the Lérin islands, there has been a monastery there for centuries.'

'Yes, that's it. Gazz said he'd take me over if there was time after Christmas.' Elodie rinsed her glass and placed it on the draining board. 'I had such a good afternoon. Oh, I forgot to ask. How was your lunch?'

'I had a good time too,' Gabby said, laughing.

Elodie enveloped her grandmother in a hug. 'Can I just say I love you and thank you for deciding to bring us here for Christmas.'

Gabby gave her a hug back, praying that when they finally

talked about the future Elodie would forgive her behaviour in the past.

'We need to put the Christmas tree lights on,' Elodie said moving away to do just that. 'And the fairy lights.'

'We also need to decide which of our festive foods we are eating tonight,' Gabby said. 'The desserts are the only thing definitely on the menu.'

'All thirteen of them,' Elodie laughed. 'Why thirteen anyway? You promised to tell me this evening.'

'They represent Jesus and the twelve disciples. Broken down into smaller sections again, the mixture of nuts, raisins and dried figs are symbolic of the four monastic orders in France, while the two sorts of nougat – white and black – stand for good and evil.' Gabby sighed. 'I think these days, though, people have largely forgotten the religious significance of the food. It's just another Christmas Eve tradition.'

'Have to admit the one I'm really looking forward to is the bûche de noel – all that chocolate and cream.' Elodie glanced at Gabby. 'Also have to admit I'm not very hungry at the moment. The pizzas were huge. Shall we not bother to cook this evening? Baguette and some pâté, some of the dessert nuts, maybe a slice of the yule log and a glass of champagne?'

'Sounds like a plan,' Gabby said. 'But if we're going to follow tradition we need to put all the desserts on the table this evening, whether we eat them or not.'

Later that evening, as they sat companionably in the sitting room enjoying a glass of champagne with their unconventional Christmas Eve meal, Elodie took a deep breath and broached the subject of No.5.

'You know you said you had to decide whether to continue letting out No.5 or sell it? There is a third option. You, me, we, could come and live in it.'

'Philippe suggested that too.'

'He did? Would you like to?'

Gabby didn't answer, instead she threw the question back at Elodie. 'Would you?'

'Of course I would. I hate my copy-editing job, my life is stuck in a rut. I would love to uproot to the south of France, who wouldn't? So can we?'

Gabby laughed. 'It's not as simple as that.'

'Why not?'

'Because these things take time to arrange, because I have a house I'd have to sell, because,' Gabby paused and stood up. 'I need to fetch something from my room.'

In her room she picked up the envelope with the hand written letter inside and hesitated. Was now the best moment? Would there ever be a better moment? Gabby took a deep breath, went back to the table and held the envelope out to Elodie.

'You need to read this.'

'What is it?' Elodie asked as she took it.

'Something you need to read. It might make moving to France difficult.'

Puzzled, Elodie looked at the postmark on the envelope. 'Who do we know in Bristol?'

Gabby didn't answer but waited for Elodie to take the letter out of the envelope, unfold it and begin to read.

Dear Gabriella and Elodie,

I'm sorry to have to tell you that my husband, Todd, died six months ago. Now everything has been dealt with I have decided to return to England. There is nothing to keep me here. I don't expect either of you to welcome me with open arms but I hope that we can meet in a civilised manner, we are, after all, the only family any of us have. I am renting a small cottage on the outskirts of Bristol while I look around for some-where more permanent. You would be welcome to come and visit me here or perhaps I could come down to Devon to see you both.

Harriet.

Elodie's hand was shaking as she held the letter out to Gabby. 'She's got a flipping nerve. Anyway, I don't see why her coming back to Europe should stop us moving to France.' Elodie stared at Gabby. 'When did you get this?'

'About three weeks ago.'

'Have you answered it?'

Gabby nodded. Knowing her daughter was back in England had brought such a surge of hope but there had been no reply to her own letter, no call to the mobile number she'd written under the address.

'I hope you told her where she could go with her "the only family any of us have" comment.'

'She's my daughter. I didn't tell her that because I'd quite like to see her again. Heal the breach between us,' Gabby said quietly. 'And I suspect she feels the same about you, after all, she is your mother.'

'She might have given birth to me but my mother she isn't. You're the only mother I've ever known. I certainly don't want to see her or have anything to do with her.' Elodie glared at Gabby. 'And neither of you can make me.'

'I know that but you—'

'As far as I'm concerned there is no but,' Elodie interrupted. 'I can understand you wanting to see her, she was in your life for over twenty years before she upped and left. I know how devas-tating that must have been for you. But, and here is a but from me, I don't have the memory of a close relationship with the woman who turned her back on us all those years ago, your daughter and my so called mother. If you want to see her and it makes you happy, fine. I'm happy without her in my life. Sorry, not sorry.'

An air of tension settled over the remainder of Christmas Eve. In desperation Gabby switched the television on but she sensed that Elodie struggled as much as she did to watch the Scandinavian crime show dubbed into French. The only thing that brought a ghost of a smile to Elodie's face was the seasonal publicity break cartoon of white chickens cavorting in the snow and knocking themselves out while skiing. Even then her smile was fleeting.

A couple of times Gabby glanced across at Elodie, wondering whether she should try talking to her again or whether it would make the situation worse. She decided to leave it. If she knew her granddaughter as well as she thought she did, Elodie would think about the letter overnight and realise her instant reaction to it had been unkind. She'd at least acknowledged that a different connection existed between her mother and her grandmother because of the time spent together in the past. That had to be regarded as a good first step.

Gabby was old enough to realise too, that the three of them would each have a lot of forgiving to do. Their reunion when it did happen, was unlikely to be a success from the word go. She anticipated a lot of treading gently around each other initially. So much to forgive. She could only hope that Elodie would eventually reach the conclusion that it was better to forgive and move on than to hold grudges. But there was one thing she was determined on. She intended to do everything possible to safeguard Elodie's future.

15

_____

After saying an early goodnight to Gabby, Elodie took a shower, hoping it would help clear her mind and help her to sleep. What a Christmas Eve. She'd been in such an upbeat mood after her trip to Valbonne with Gazz. On the drive back, as she'd leant into him, her arms hugging him around his waist, something that felt so natural she'd dared to dream that they could do things like this together in the future. She'd been all fired up to persuade Gabby that it was a brilliant idea for them both to move into No.5 as soon as possible in the new year. Then Gabby had produced the letter and instantly Elodie had regressed to being the angry teenage girl who had come to hate her mother for abandoning her for a man.

And now the death of that man had blown new life onto the long dead embers of that anger. How dare her mother assume she could waltz back into their lives and become one happy family again – if they had ever been a happy family in the first place. Years ago there had been so many questions Elodie wanted answered. Now, she couldn't remember them because neither the questions nor the answers had any importance in her life any longer. Time had erased the harsh necessity of desperately wanting to know, turning it instead into a resigned acceptance of it was life, things happen. But that didn't mean she had to welcome the mother who had abandoned her back in her own life after such a long absence, or be forced to share her grandmother's affection with her.

As for Gabby, she seemed almost happy at the prospect of seeing her daughter again. A daughter whose actions had severely changed the middle course of her life when she'd foisted responsibility for Elodie on to her. Had Gabby's motto always been forgive and forget? Probably. Elodie had never known her to be intentionally unkind to anyone. Being kind could be described as her default setting.

She sat on her bed, deep in thought. Ever since they decided to spend Christmas and the New Year in Juan-les-Pins she'd been excited. Not just because Gabby wanted to actually celebrate her birthday for once but that she wanted to do it in her home town. It didn't matter that it would still only be the two of them, it would be memorable by virtue of the place they were in.

When Gabby had shown her around No.5, Elodie had allowed the idea of moving to France to seep into her brain. Earlier, when she'd mentioned the idea of them both moving to France and living in the villa as a wonderful opportunity to change her life, Gabby hadn't dismissed it. She'd simply produced *that letter* and waited for her reaction. Why should the re-appearance of the woman who'd abandoned them both stop Gabby and her from upping sticks and moving over here? In fact, if her mother was going to be living in the UK she definitely would prefer to move to another country.

But if Gabby was prepared to welcome her only daughter into her life, then she, Elodie, would have to accept it because the last thing she wanted to do was hurt or upset her grandmother. In no way though, did that mean she was going to play happy families with her mother anytime soon. Elodie sighed as she snuggled down under the duvet. Polite but distant was the way to go, she decided as she switched off the bedside light.

Christmas Day dawned and Elodie, to her grandmother's relief when she got up, was already in the kitchen preparing their traditional Christmas breakfast: scrambled eggs on toast and a glass each of bucks fizz. Years ago, for fun, Gabby had made a pair of short quilted stockings from material with Christmas trees, robins and snowmen printed on it, ready to be filled with small gifts every Christmas. This morning, Elodie had already placed one of the stockings on the table in front of her grand-mother's usual chair and Gabby placed the other stocking on the table for Elodie before turning and holding out her arms for a hug. They both said 'Happy Christmas.' at the same time as they hugged.

Elodie said. 'Eggs will be ready in five. Help yourself to a bucks fizz. And then we can dive into the stockings before breakfast.'

Both the stockings had more of a French flavour than usual this year. Gabby's with some Marseille lavender soap, a French pocket size diary, an enamelled brooch in the shape of a cigale, a packet of mints and a single macaroon in a presentation box.

Elodie laughed when she saw her stocking also had a bar of Marseille soap in amongst the other presents, 'Great minds.' As well as the soap there was a creamy coloured soft velvet scarf, a paperback of Scott Fitzgerald's *Tender Is The Night*, a fun pair of holly earrings that flashed when pressed and a packet of LU chocolate biscuits that had rapidly become a favourite since she'd picked up her first packet in the supermarket.

Elodie picked up the paperback. 'I love this book. My old copy at home is falling apart.'

Gabby nodded. 'I noticed. Fitzgerald spent a lot of time in Juan-les-Pins in the nineteen-twenties. Although *Tender is The Night* wasn't published until the mid nineteen-thirties some years after he left the Riviera, I thought you might like to re-read it in the town where the Jazz Age and the company he kept influenced his writing.'

'After we've opened the presents under the tree, are we going for a walk like we do at home?' Elodie asked as they tucked into their eggs.

'Yes. Along the front for some fresh sea breezes and then back to prepare lunch. Not that we have much to prepare this year as we decided against a full roast,' Gabby said.

Breakfast over, dishwasher loaded, Elodie made for the tree in the sitting room where the presents they'd bought each other were nestled side by side.

Elodie handed Gabby hers. 'I know we agreed on token presents only this year but I couldn't resist buying this for you.'

Gabby was delighted with the figurine of the snowy owl with its real feathers that Elodie had found in the Christmas market. 'It's small enough to go in your suitcase safely when we leave,' she said.

Elodie loved her notebook with its embossed cover and accompanying pen that Gabby had given her. 'It's almost too nice to write in,' she said, stroking the cover. 'But I will.'

It was almost mid-morning when they both grabbed a jacket and set off on their walk. The town was quieter than normal with some shops and cafés closed but the restaurants that were open were busy. They walked further along the bord de mer in the direction of Golfe Juan than Elodie had been before. The sea front was lined with several apartment blocks with shops and more cafés at pavement level. Elodie saw a small jetty just as they turned to go back and wondered if it was the one where Gazz's new business was based.

They'd been back at the apartment for an hour or so, busy preparing the vegetables for lunch when the large elephant circling around them that they'd both successfully avoided mentioning all morning, waved its trunk in Elodie's face. Gabby had placed three duck breasts in the oven tray and set the table for three people.

'Why three breasts and three places?' Elodie asked, surprised. 'Are we expecting a guest? Oh, have you invited Philippe?'

Gabby seized on her question gratefully. 'I just suggested if he was free and fancied joining us for lunch he'd be more than welcome but he did say Mickaël and Jessica would expect him to spend the day with them so it was unlikely he'd be free to join us. I left it open ended.'

She turned away quickly and started to fold the serviettes, convinced that if Elodie caught a glimpse of her face she'd know she was lying. But something in her voice must have alerted Elodie.

'It's not Philippe you've invited, is it? Did you tell a certain person we were down here for Christmas?'

Gabby nodded. 'Yes. But as I told you last night I haven't heard from her so it's unlikely she'll come.'

'So why lay a place at the table then?'

'Just in case she does turn up. Make her feel she was expected and is welcome.'

'Not by me she's not.'

'Please Elodie, let's not fight today, of all days,' Gabby said.

Elodie took a deep breath. Christmas was supposed to be a happy time. A time when families got together and enjoyed themselves. Not tear themselves apart. 'You're right. We won't let her spoil Christmas for us when she's not even here.' And she smiled a bright smile that didn't quite reach her eyes.

Much to Elodie's relief, lunch passed without anybody arriving and she was able to relax. She should have known that Harriet would be a no show – since when had she put herself out for either her mother or her own daughter?

The two of them spent the rest of the day contentedly reading, listening to music and enjoying the chocolates and other treats they'd bought to indulge in.

After loading their plates for supper and before closing the fridge door, Gabby looked at the remaining charcuterie, the cheeses and the unopened packets of pâté they had bought from the delicatessen counter in the supermarket.

'We're never going to eat all this. Shall we invite Jessica and everyone down for a Boxing Day lunch tomorrow? The French don't celebrate it as such but I'm sure Jessica will remember it growing up.'

'Good idea,' Elodie said, hoping that Gazz would be free to come with his parents as well.

'One of us can go up in the morning and ask them,' Gabby said. 'We will need to buy another bottle or two of champagne if they can come.'

16

It was Elodie who went up to the penthouse apartment the next morning and issued the invitation. Jessica accepted instantly on everyone's behalf. 'What a lovely idea. I used to love Boxing Day with its laid back party atmosphere. We'll see you at midday.'

Gabby volunteered to go to the supermarket for the extra champagne and to pick up a couple of fresh baguettes, some crisps, another yule log and a packet of festive serviettes. Elodie gave the sitting room a quick tidy and vacuum with the machine she found in the cupboard, plumped up the cushions, switched on the tree and the other fairy lights and found the classical music channel on the television again.

She was in the kitchen sorting out glasses and small plates ready to carry them through to the table in the sitting room when Gabby returned. Between them they cut up the baguettes and put various toppings on them: ham, cheese, pâté and cold duck slices. Crisps were emptied into bowls, olives were put in small dishes and the champagne was put in the fridge alongside the new yule log.

Elodie's welcoming smile when she opened the door at twelve

o'clock to greet everyone, faltered slightly when she saw Fiona clutching Gazz's arm.

'Hope you don't mind me gate-crashing,' Fiona said. 'Gazz said you wouldn't. Only he's taking me to Monaco for the afternoon and evening so I thought I'd come over this morning and treat him to lunch before we leave, instead, he's dragged me here.'

'No problem. Nice to see you again. Are you going to Monaco on the scooter?' Elodie asked looking at Gazz standing at Fiona's side. Before he could answer Fiona exclaimed.

'Of course not!' she shuddered. 'I hate that scooter. Gazz knows I wouldn't dream of getting on it. Jessica has kindly lent us her car.'

Elodie decided against mentioning how much she'd loved her scooter ride the other day, instead, she smiled and offered them both glasses of champagne before she turned away. The friendly Gazz who had been such fun company in Valbonne seemed to have disappeared. Fiona was definitely calling the shots today.

Philippe had made a beeline for Gabby and the two of them were already laughing at something one or other of them had said.

Jessica and Mickaël were looking around the apartment in amazement. 'I love all the lights. And the throw. You've made it so Christmassy,' Jessica said.

'I hope you don't mind,' Elodie said, feeling awkward. It was Jessica's apartment after all. 'I got a bit carried away. We'll take them down, obviously, when we leave. I haven't fixed anything to anything.'

Jessica waved her concerns away. 'Don't worry. This all looks delicious,' she said, moving across to the table where the food was. 'I love pâté and crisps. I rarely buy either because I can't stop eating them, so I go mad for them at Christmastime when I indulge myself.' She glanced across at Gabby who was talking to Philippe.

'Philippe has really perked up since he met your grandmother. He's been a bit down since the operation. He says Gabby owns a house down here?'

'She does. I'm trying to persuade her that we should both come down here to live.'

'D'you think that will happen?'

Elodie shrugged. 'There's a bit of a problem that has to be sorted before that can happen but, fingers crossed it will, because I really want to.' She glanced across to make sure Gabby was still talking with Philippe before leaning in to Jessica and whispering.

'It's Gabby's birthday on New Year's Eve and I'm going organise a surprise tea party for her. Not sure where yet but would you like to come? And the others, of course.'

'We'd love to. Let me know when and where and the four of us will be there. And the two of you are invited upstairs in the evening for supper and to watch the fireworks. We decided not to have a party this year but we'll definitely stay up to see the New Year in.'

'Oh, that will be a lovely, thank you.'

'But first we have the next few days to get through,' Jessica sighed. 'I always think of the days between Christmas and New Year as being a bit of a turkey week when nothing much happens.'

Elodie looked at her. 'Never heard it called that before.'

'My father was a vicar so I grew up with lots of little moral tales from the bible. The turkey one relates to Job who lost his possessions and wellbeing to test his faith.' Jessica shrugged. 'Christmas is over, we've all spent too much, eaten too much and there's nothing to do while we're all waiting for the 'wonderful'

New Year to kick off. There's a sort of parallel there, in my mind if not in anybody else's.'

'I agree it's definitely a something and nothing few days,' Elodie said. 'From now on I shall always refer to it as the turkey week.'

Gazz wandered over on his own, at that moment, leaving Fiona talking to Mickaël. Elodie smiled at him and was happy to receive one in return.

'I wanted to apologise for Fiona gate-crashing and to say we'll be leaving soon.'

'It's not a problem. Enjoy your afternoon in Monaco,' Elodie said. 'It's on my list to visit. Probably not this week but the next time we're down.'

'I'll be back down here when you come again and I'd be more than happy to take you and show you around,' Gazz said.

'Won't you be too busy running your new business?' Elodie felt her heart skip a beat at the thought of spending time with Gazz in the future.

'Told you about that has he?' Jessica said. 'Why he feels the need to throw away a good career is beyond his father and me but,' she shook her head. 'We'll do all we can to help.'

'Appreciated maman.' Gazz kissed his mother's cheek.

'And Fiona's not happy about it either. She might say she's looking forward to seeing more of you but she's worried you'll be broke if it doesn't work out.'

'It's nothing to do with Fiona,' Gazz said. 'And my new business will work out. You'll see.'

17

The next morning Elodie was up early and went to buy their breakfast croissants from their regular boulangerie. Standing in the queue, waiting to be served, she wondered where the nearest boulangerie was to No.5. This one was good but was quite a distance away from the villa. She'd noticed as they'd explored there was no shortage of either boulangeries or pharmacies in Juan – there appeared to be one or the other on nearly every corner so there was sure to be one close to No.5.

She wandered along the sea front back to the apartment clutching her bag of croissants and planning to ask Gabby if they could visit the villa again. Elodie pressed the button for the lift in the foyer and stepped back in surprise when Philippe stepped out as its doors opened.

'Bonjour, Philippe. You're out and about early.'

Philippe pulled a face. 'Rendez-vous with my doctor, best to get it over and done with early in the day. I hear there's a surprise birthday party soon? Is it a special one for Gabby? Mind you, at our age, every birthday is special.'

Elodie smiled. 'Yes, it's the big seven O but I'm still not sure where it will be. I thought about the Belles Rives but I think it's a little bit out of my price range for a champagne tea party. And I'm not sure Gabby would feel terribly comfortable there either. I may end up holding it in the apartment.'

'I know the perfect place for afternoon tea. Gabby already likes it there. Leave it with me. I'll book it this morning and confirm it with you later. D'accord?'

Elodie beamed him a smile. 'Really? There will be six of us if the place you know needs numbers.'

Philippe waved his hand in the air. 'Six or sixteen, it matters not. Ah, my taxi arrives. I'll see you later.'

As Elodie entered the apartment, Gabby came out of her bedroom. 'Coffee is ready to go. I thought we'd sit on the balcony for breakfast, it's another gorgeous morning.'

'And we have another week here. I'm so happy you insisted on booking this place for a fortnight,' Elodie said. 'Any chance we can go take another look at the villa today, please?' She felt Gabby tense and waited for her to turn down the idea.

'Yes, if you want to. I have my meeting with the agent tomorrow – another visit might help clear my mind.'

Passing a boulangerie on the way to the villa, Elodie insisted on buying a couple of cakes and two takeaway coffees.

'I want to sit in the garden and dream about living there,' she said.

Gabby smiled and shook her head but said she'd love an apricot slice.

This time, when they got to the villa, Elodie opened the shutters on all the French doors leading out into the garden and surveyed the room again, admiring the large inset fire in the granite fireplace.

'I bet this room looked wonderful at Christmas. Where did you have the tree?'

'In front of the middle pair of French doors. We rarely opened those in winter.' Gabby said. 'Come on, that coffee isn't going to get any warmer. Let's find somewhere to sit in the garden and drink it.'

Between them they pulled a couple of chairs out of the pool house and set them up on the paved terrace in front of the French windows facing the pool. 'The green's not exactly inviting, is it?' Elodie commented, sipping her coffee.

'The tenants obviously cancelled the pool boy before they left.' Gabby said. 'Which is annoying. I'll have to pay for it to be cleaned before it can be let out again.'

'How about before we move in?' Elodie teased. A silence of about ten seconds followed her words before Gabby responded.

'I have been thinking about moving here and I've decided I'm not going to sell the house.'

'So can we come and live here – early in the new year?' Elodie turned and looked at her hopefully.

Gabby shook her head. 'Early in the new year is probably not feasible. Let's just say sometime in the future we will come to live down here. Sorting certain things out will take time, so rather than have the place standing empty, I'm going to instruct the agent to carry on letting it out but on short term contracts of three months only.'

Elodie sighed. Not what she wanted to hear, but at least Gabby had agreed that they would eventually move down here, so that was something. Now all she had to do was persuade her that one, three month contract, would be enough time to sort everything out and they could start making plans to move down in time for summer on the Riviera next year.

18

Harriet Rogers stood to one side out of the way of the crowds surging back and forth on the concourse of Nice Côte d'Azur airport and took a couple of deep, steadying breaths. Todd had always taken control of any journeys they made, checking and working out the best route, booking any flights or hotels that were necessary, whilst she organised the house and did the packing for both of them. It had always worked like clockwork in the main. Travelling alone took her way out of her comfort zone these days and now she was here on French soil the tension throughout her body had increased. She'd hoped that this, only the second time of travelling without Todd at her side and being a shorter journey, it would be easier than the journey back to England had been. If anything though, it was harder, probably because of the knots that had gathered in her stomach the moment the decision had been made to come down here. There was only one reason for her to be here, the inevitable family reunion. A reunion that could go either way, Harriet felt. The truth was, she had no idea of the reception she was likely to receive and that worry gnawed away at those knots non stop.

Reading her mother's reply to her letter, she appeared to be positively looking forward to their reunion, but Elodie's likely reaction was impossible to predict. In recent years Elodie had stopped writing directly to her, leaving it to Gabby. Harriet had assumed from this that it was Elodie's way of showing how hurt she was at being left behind all those years ago and the easiest way of showing this, was to ignore her mother.

Would Elodie even be prepared to listen to her explanation as to why she'd behaved as she did all those years ago, let alone forgive her selfish actions? All she knew was she had to try and hope, pray, that there would be some semblance of understanding from her daughter. That maybe, if not forgiveness, at least some sympathetic compassion, even if she didn't deserve it.

Standing there as the crowds of passengers ebbed and flowed around her, Harriet pulled herself together. The last part of the journey would be easier. In recent weeks she'd read all the travel guides she could lay her hands on and knew that now all she had to decide was whether to catch a bus that would take time to travel along the coast making frequent stops, or take a taxi to her hotel which would be quicker, if more expensive.

She could see the taxi rank to her right, there were a few people waiting. A sudden desire to simplify and finish the journey quickly hit her. To hell with the cost. She could afford it anyway. Taking a taxi straight to the hotel would be much easier. She trundled her suitcase along and joined the queue. Five minutes later she was giving the name of her hotel to the driver of the second taxi to draw up and speeding away from the airport towards Antibes.

The taxi dropped her outside the modern, functional hotel she'd chosen from the internet and where she was booked in until the New Year, and drove away. Inside, the hotel the receptionist welcomed her, signed her in, handed over the pass card for the door and pointed her in the direction of the lift to the third floor.

Once in the room, Harriet abandoned her suitcase, opened the patio doors and stepped out onto the small balcony, where she stood looking out to sea and taking gulping breaths of the salty air as traffic passed on the road below.

Now she was here she was beginning to wonder if jumping on a plane and coming down here was actually the right thing to do. Arranging to meet in the UK in the New Year would have been far less stressful. Instead, she'd seized on her mother's invitation to meet up in Juan-les-Pins as an encouraging sign. But then she'd chickened out of turning up for Christmas, opting instead to arrive a day or so before Gabby's birthday, telling herself that travelling over Christmas would be horrendous. And why had she thought simply turning up out of the blue would be a good idea? Was she hoping to wrongfoot Gabby and Elodie, giving her the advantage of surprise? Good manners indicated she should have, at least, answered the letter, or rung the mobile number that had been written under the address. Which she still could, of course. Perhaps Elodie was organising a celebration for her grandmother? If she turned up at a birthday party then the chances were that her presence would hijack the occasion and she'd become the centre of attention as the woman who'd abandoned both her daughter and her mother. She couldn't spoil such a special birthday for Gabby. Maybe it would be better to have the first meeting before then.

Several minutes had passed before she stepped back inside, closed the balcony doors, shutting out the outside world and all its possible complications. She crossed to the small fridge and discovered that the mini bar contained a small bottle of gin and a bottle of tonic. Just what she needed. Drinking slowly, Harriet acknowledged to herself that her biggest problem was likely to be Elodie. The child she'd left behind and with whom she was desperate to reconnect with all these years later and try to make amends, if possible.

19

The next day Gabby dressed carefully for her rendez-vous with Monsieur Albrecht. She'd toyed with the idea of asking Philippe to accompany her before deciding against it. It was just a business meeting, all she had to remember was that the agent was actually working for her, not the other way around.

The receptionist's jolly Christmas hat had been discarded but she did give Gabby a friendly smile when she walked in.

'Monsieur Albrecht said to bring you straight in when you arrived. Can I get you a coffee or tea? No. Come this way then.' She led the way to a half open door and opening it fully, introduced her. 'Madame Jacques is here,' and ushered Gabby into the room before drawing the door carefully closed behind her.

To Gabby's surprise there were two men in the office and they got to their feet and greeted her politely, the older one offering her a chair as he introduced himself.

'Pascal Albrecht. It's good to meet you after all this time,' he said. 'This is Jean-Frances Moulin. I thought it would be a good idea to introduce the two of you, especially as you will be returning to England soon.'

'Why is it a good idea?'

'Because I always like to see the person I'm doing business with,' Jean-Frances said smoothly.

'But I'm not doing business with you,' Gabby said, turning to him. 'My appointment is with Monsieur Albrecht and the fact that you are here is most irregular.'

'I'm hoping that you will be doing business with me. I want to buy your villa. I think Pascal has told you I am interested.'

'He said there had been some interest but no names and no figure was mentioned. And, quite honestly, I hadn't thought about selling.' Gabby looked at the man whom she instinctively distrusted, straight in the eyes. 'But, out of curiosity, what figure do you have in mind?'

'Ten per cent over market value.'

Gabby pulled a face. 'No, I don't think so.'

'Fifteen per cent then.'

Gabby regarded him for several seconds before shaking her head. 'Better, but it's still no.'

'Name the figure you will consider accepting,' said Jean-Frances, his eyes narrowing.

Gabby took a deep breath and decided to face him down. 'There isn't one. No.5 is not for sale. Or for rent. But I am intrigued as to why you'd be willing to pay so much for it?' There was silence as she stared at him, waiting for his answer.

'I didn't think you'd tell me. Right. You two clearly have something going on here to which I'm not a party.'

She turned to face the estate agent who was looking visibly uncomfortable. 'Monsieur Albrecht. The tenants have moved out of my house. There is no rental agreement in place, therefore there is no contract between us. I am free to take my business elsewhere. Correct?' She raised her eyebrows at him as he visibly squirmed before giving her a nod.

'In that case, I thank you for past services and I'd like you to give me back all the keys you hold for my property.'

'That's not necessary, surely? I think you're over reacting. All I was doing was introducing you to a buyer for your property. If you prefer to keep letting it out, I can continue to handle that for you.'

Gabby shook her head. 'I don't think so. Besides, I've decided now would be a good time to move back here to live, so I have no further need of your agency.' She held out her hand. 'My keys please, now.'

Monsieur Albrecht pressed the intercom button on his desk. 'Please bring all the keys to Madame Jacques' property in here immediately.'

Gabby could feel Jean-Frances' eyes boring into her while they waited in a silence that she had no intention of breaking and neither, it seemed, did either of the men standing there staring at her. When, a minute later, the receptionist came in carrying the keys, Gabby held out her hand again. 'Thank you. I'll take them.'

Jean-Frances stared at her as he said quietly. 'I do hope you don't regret turning down my offer, Madame Jacques.'

'I do hope that you are not suggesting I might have reason to, Monsieur Moulin? In which case, I'm sure I won't.' Gabby said. 'Goodbye.' She turned and left the room.

The receptionist looked at her questioningly as she walked past her desk as they both heard the raised angry voices in the office. 'Everything is all okay for you?' she asked.

Gabby stopped and looked at her. 'Oui, for me it is all good. I'm not sure whether you know what was supposed to happen in today's meeting but I'm afraid those two gentlemen pushed their luck with me,' she said. The receptionist looked at her blankly.

'Pushed their luck?'

Remembering a well known phrase from her childhood,

Gabby leant in and said quietly, 'Faut pas pousser Mamie dans les orties,' she said, and the receptionist smothered a laugh at her words. 'Grandma must not be pushed into the nettles.'

Once outside Gabby felt the adrenaline that had fired her up in the office, drain away leaving her shaking and she had to force herself to put one foot in front of the other. She hadn't gone more than a couple of metres when she met Philippe.

'I timed that well, didn't I?' he said cheerfully. 'I thought we could have coffee together this morning.' He gave her a worried look as he realised she was shaking. 'Gabriella, what's wrong? What's happened?'

'I could really do with that coffee,' she said. 'And then I'll tell you.'

Sitting at a pavement café in one of the back streets of Juan, Gabby sipped a strong expresso that Philippe insisted she put a small spoonful of sugar in and gradually stopped shaking. Philippe waited patiently until she was ready to talk.

He gazed at her, horrified, as she told him about her meeting with Albrecht and Moulin. 'It doesn't make sense to me. No.5 is one of eight perfectly nice but ordinary detached suburban villas in that cul-de sac. Do you have any idea why Moulin would offer me so much money for it?'

Philippe fingered his chin thoughtfully. 'No, but I'm certainly going to ask around. See if I can find out. So, you've got the keys back, what now? When are you coming to live in it?'

Gabby shook her head. 'I think that was a bit of an impulsive reaction to what the two of them were suggesting. My way of closing down the conversation and getting out of there. I told Elodie yesterday I had decided to let it on short term contracts, whilst sorting out things in England. But now, of course, I need to find another agent to handle the rental side of things. Can you recommend another agent for me?'

Philippe shook his head at her. 'Truly? Be honest with yourself, Gabriella. I think you telling Albrecht you were moving back was your subconscious giving you a kick into admitting the truth to yourself. You want to come here to live sooner rather than later.'

Gabby closed her eyes and rubbed her face before giving a deep sigh and looking at him. 'Yes, I do. But I have to sell my house in Devon and that will take a couple of months. And,' she hesitated. 'I feel I need to be in the UK for at least a few months now Harriet has returned. Being in the same country, it would be easier to get to know each other again. I know it's only a short plane ride but there's a couple of other problems too. Elodie is very anti her mother currently, which makes me sad and I would like to see them grow closer. I also need to sort out the inheritance problem now that Harriet has turned up again.'

'Now that I can help you with,' Philippe said. 'I'll introduce you to my notaire and my financial advisor. Problems can be solved with the right advice.'

'Oh, Philippe, you make it all sound so easy. I admit I do feel a strong urge to come back home. I've loved being here for the last week and I'm not looking forward to leaving in the New Year. I just wish things between the three of us weren't in such a desperate state. It complicates things.'

Philippe caught hold of her hand and squeezed it. 'It can be easier than you expect. Carpe Diem. Do what will make you happy by seizing the day and going for it. Elodie and Harriet will find their own way. Most things have a habit of working themselves out given the chance.'

Gabby nodded thoughtfully. 'I guess you are right. I was

hoping that Harriet would come for Christmas but that was probably a bit of wishful thinking on my part.'

'So, have I convinced you enough to take the plunge and come back? Sooner rather than later?' Philippe said, turning as his attention was caught by a woman stepping off the pavement a few yards away from them into the path of a cyclist who narrowly avoided running into her. The woman held up her hands in apology as she backed away from the angry torrent of French the man directed at her.

'I'll talk to Elodie and oh,' Gabby's voice froze as she too looked and saw the woman who was now hurrying by on the opposite side of the road.

'Gabriella, what is the matter?' Philippe asked.

'That woman? It's Harriet. I'd recognise that walk of hers anywhere. I need to catch her up,' and Gabby went to stand up and run across the road.

Philippe put out a restraining hand. 'Don't. I saw her reaction as she noticed us, you, sitting here. I think that's why she stepped out without looking. She panicked because she recognised you as easily as you did her. If she'd wanted to talk to you, she had the opportunity to stop. Instead, she walked away. It would be better to let her decide to contact you when she is ready.'

As Harriet disappeared out of sight, Gabby sank back down on her chair, trying to hold the tears at bay. 'But if she's in France, that must mean she came with the intention of contacting me, doesn't it?'

Philippe nodded. 'Yes, but I think she still needs time and it needs to be on her terms, a chance meeting would be out of her control. Especially as you weren't alone.'

20

Gabby and Philippe walked slowly back to the apartment. Philippe, using the excuse he'd forgotten his stick, to take Gabby's arm for support, but in reality she was more than happy to have his arm threaded through hers.

As the lift doors opened on Gabby's floor, Philippe gave her a gentle goodbye kiss on the cheek. 'Don't worry about Harriet and tell Elodie your decision right away. And please also tell Elodie I got that information she wanted some help with if she wants to pop up. See you soon.'

Elodie was in the sitting room working on her laptop and looked up as Gabby opened the door.

'How did you get on at the agency? Did they agree to a short three month tenancy, or did they try to convince you six month ones were a better option?'

'No rental contract ever again with that agency. The person who wants to buy the villa was there and told me to name my price.' Gabby looked at Elodie with her eyebrows raised.

'Please tell me you haven't agreed to sell after all?' Elodie said, a note of despair in her voice.

'To their annoyance I turned all their offers down and told them I intended to live there with immediate effect and I'd like my keys returned.'

Elodie interrupted with a shriek of delight and leapt up to give her grandmother a hug. 'Seriously? You're not going to let it out any more. We can come and live in No.5 in the New Year?'

Gabby nodded as she put two sets of keys on the table.

'If you're sure it's what you want.'

'I do I do I do. This is turning out to be the best Christmas ever.'

'I met Philippe afterwards and he said to tell you that he has the info you were asking about. If you'd like to pop up he'll give it to you.' She glanced at Elodie curiously but Elodie simply smiled at her.

'Great news. I'll pop up now.'

'There's something else you need to know. Your mother is in town,' Gabby said quietly.

Elodie stopped by the door.

'You've spoken to her? What did she have to say?'

'Nothing. Philippe and I were having a coffee when I saw her but she didn't see me.' No point in telling Elodie that Harriet had avoided speaking to her, it would only fuel more bad feeling.

'I bet she did see you and deliberately avoided making contact. I'm going up to see Philippe.' and Elodie closed the door behind her.

Gabby sighed. Elodie could be too perceptive at times. She and Elodie were here for another week. How long was Harriet staying? Would she make contact before they returned to the UK? Or would she leave without bothering?

* * *

Harriet had been enjoying exploring Juan-les-Pins before she saw Gabby sitting at the pavement café with a man. Their body language was relaxed and comfortable, the man listening attentively to something her mother was saying. Seeing her mother with a man threw Harriet for some reason she couldn't fathom. She'd never envisaged Gabby with anyone other than her father in all the years she'd been away.

Was it a man she'd just met? A French friend from the days when Gabby had called France home? Had her mother remarried? Surely she would have mentioned it in one of their infrequent letters? But there again, why would she? Those letters, on both sides, had tended to gloss over certain things and to be economical with the truth about others. Harriet knew this because she was guilty of employing those tactics herself.

Of course she could have, should have, stopped and spoken to Gabby. Instead, instinctively after that incident with the cyclist, she'd bent her head and scurried across the road. She was too shaken after that to talk to her mother. Besides, meeting up with her mother for the first time in so many years had to be done in private, not in the presence of an onlooker. She could only hope that Gabby hadn't noticed her and wouldn't be hurt, thinking she'd been ignored.

Deep in thought, Harriet wandered aimlessly through a maze of back streets before finally finding herself on the far end of Juan-les-Pins promenade where she turned with relief in the direction of her hotel. Passing an empty bench, she sat for some time staring out at the sea. She'd come all this way to see, to talk to both her mother and her daughter. If she was too frightened to do that because she was worried about the reception she would get, she might as well catch the next flight out of Nice and go back to the UK. Leave it until the New Year before they met. Harriet took out her phone and then put it away again. She'd text Gabby later when she felt steadier and suggest they met for lunch tomorrow. No, she'd just suggest they met. Gabby was the one person who could tell her how Elodie was likely to react, how she should approach things. If all went well the two of them could decide about lunch afterwards. But where to meet up?

* * *

Elodie ran up the stairs to the penthouse rather than take the lift. She needed to expel some of her pent up anger at the thought of Harriet ignoring Gabby. Gazz answered the door to her knock, his face lighting up with a smile when he saw her.

'Hi.'

'Hi. I've come up to see Philippe,' she said, smiling back. Gazz opened the door wider.

'Come on in. My granddad gets all the ladies. What's he got that I haven't?'

'Just some information I need,' Elodie said. 'He was asking at a restaurant that Gabby likes whether they could cater for her birthday.'

'The answer is, yes, they can,' Philippe said, appearing in the hallway. 'Afternoon tea with champagne is booked for four o'clock on the thirty-first. They'd like the party to finish by six thirty, at the latest, so they can prepare for a busy evening.'

'Brilliant,' Elodie said. 'Two and half hours is fine. Just one thing – where is it?'

'Here's their card. You can go check it out if you want to.'

'Thank you so much.'

'My pleasure. How is Gabriella now? Her morning was quite a stressful one.'

'She seems fine, a bit quiet.' Elodie said. 'I'm so pleased she's decided to keep and move into the house because that means I get to live in the south of France too. Can't wait.'

Philippe nodded. 'And she's not still upset over your mother?'

'Gabby told me she'd seen Harriet and that Harriet didn't see her. But she did, didn't she?'

Philippe gave a reluctant nod.

'And chose to ignore her as I suspected. No wonder Gabby was quiet. If you only knew how much I hate that woman for the hurt she's caused Gabby.'

'But she's Gabby's daughter and she still loves her,' Philippe said. 'And she's your mother,'

Elodie shook her head quickly. 'Not in any true sense of that word. Gabby has been my mother for the last twenty years. Harriet, by walking away and leaving, forfeited the right to the name. And she needn't think I want her in my life now, because I don't. Excuse me,' and Elodie left the two men before they could see the tears streaking down her face.

21

After her morning shower, Gabby gazed again at the text message she'd heard ping in at 3 a.m. as sleep evaded her. She'd read it then with a sense of relief and the same sense of relief flooded through her as she read it a second time. She guessed Philippe had been right. Harriet needed to feel in charge of their first meeting but she was finally admitting she was here and willing to talk. Gabby smiled at the directions in the text:

11 a.m. in the park where they hold the jazz festival. Sorry, can't remember the name. Pinède something.

Still the same Harriet then, she never could remember the names of places or people.

Quickly Gabby typed a reply:

I'll be there.

Standing in front of the bedroom window holding her phone she thought about telling Elodie and decided against it. She'd tell her afterwards when she'd discovered how Harriet was and what her plans were – and how she reacted to being told how hostile her own daughter was to her returning. Gabby was determined though, not to stand by and see Elodie hurt by her mother a second time. Harriet needed to be equally unwavering in her determination to stay in Elodie's life this time. Not run away again.

Gabby heard the apartment door open and close and Elodie call out, 'Croissant delivery.'

Sitting eating their breakfast out on the balcony, Elodie sighed. 'I'm so looking forward to having breakfast on the terrace of No.5.'

'That won't happen for a few weeks yet,' Gabby said. 'So much to do before then.'

'Has No.5 ever had a name?' Elodie pulled her croissant apart and looked at her grandmother. 'Because I think we should give it one. Just a number is not enough for such a beautiful villa. Besides, it's a new era for it and us.'

Gabby shook her head in amusement at Elodie. 'Fine. Have a think about names. We can have a plaque made for the gate pillar when we move in.' She placed her coffee mug on the table. 'What are you up to today?'

'I'm going to try and catch up with some writing, ready to start pitching the magazines early in the New Year. Thought I'd see if there would be any interest too, in a regular column from a newbie in the south of France. Once I've caught up with all that I'll go shopping. We need some more coffee if nothing else.'

'I can do that,' Gabby said. 'Shall we eat out tonight?'

Elodie smiled. 'Yes. Soak up a bit more atmosphere.'

* * *

Gabby couldn't see Harriet at first when she walked down to La Pinède Gould and her heart sank. Had she changed her mind; couldn't face meeting after all? Maybe she was just late, Gabby thought hopefully as she walked slowly along and then she saw her.

Harriet was meandering, head down, along the Jazz Walk of Fame, absorbed in the handprints of famous jazz musicians set in plaques into the pavement. Gabby watched her for a few moments, drinking in her outward appearance without being noticed. Wearing white jeans and a pink silk shirt, her figure slim and with her auburn hair in a messy up do Gabby could still see the young woman who had defied her all those years ago and left to live her own life far away. Had it been as good as she'd expected? Had regret caught up with her at some point? Gabby was about to find out.

'Hello, Harriet,' she said quietly, standing at her side, wanting to throw her arms around her in a tight hug but not sure how welcome this would be.

'Mum,' Harriet said. 'I didn't see you arrive.' She hesitated before leaning in and kissing Gabby on the cheek. 'It's good to see you.'

'How are you?' Gabby asked, concerned at how tired Harriet looked now she was closer.

'I'm okay. How are you?'

'I'm fine, getting old, of course, but happy to see you. Shall we walk? Or shall we sit here,' Gabby indicated a bench. 'We can get a drink and watch the activity in the small animals farm over there in the garden. We've got so much to catch up on.'

'Let's do that,' Harriet said.

'Hot chocolate okay?' When Harriet nodded her thanks, Gabby left her sitting on the bench whilst she went to get the drinks.

'Do they set this up just for Christmas every year?' Harriet asked, when Gabby returned.

'I have no idea, this is the first time I've spent Christmas here for a long time, but it seems popular so I guess they do. Pony rides are always popular with young girls,' Gabby said, as they both watched a young girl being lifted up to sit on a skewbald pony.

'I regret so much not seeing Elodie grow up,' Harriet said quietly. 'There hasn't been a day when I haven't missed her, regretted leaving her behind, although I suspect she'll find that hard to believe.' She took several sips of her drink before speaking again.

'Mum, I have to confess something. I saw you yesterday and because you were with a man, I chickened out from acknowledging you. I wanted our first meeting to be more than accidental.'

'I know. I saw you too. I was all for coming after you, but Philippe persuaded me not to. He said you probably needed more time and wanted a private meeting.'

'He was right. Who is he?'

'He's a very new friend who somehow already generates the aura of being an old friend. I like him a lot,' Gabby added quietly. 'He has a gentle positive outlook to life these days, although he admits his son was right to call him a bit of a reprobate in the past. I'm sure you'll like him when you meet him.'

'Why did you come to France this year?' Harriet said.

'A couple of reasons but basically after forty years of being away, I wanted to see the place again. I guess I was homesick. You?'

'Me?'

'Why return to England now and not before? You could have come with Todd. Why wait until he died?'

Harriet was silent before she took a long sip of her hot chocolate. 'Because he didn't want to come and he wouldn't let me come alone.' She glanced at Gabby. 'He knew that I was unlikely to return to him if I came back home alone.'

'Was your marriage unhappy?'

When Harriet bit her lip and didn't answer, Gabby glanced at her sharply. 'Was it? Please don't tell me he was violent towards you?'

'No, never violent, but he controlled everything I did. And now the irony is, I'm lost without someone telling me what to do, what to think, where to go. In short, I'm the pathetic woman he always told me I was but to answer your question, yes, my marriage did indeed turn into an unhappy one.'

'Oh, Harriet, you were never ever pathetic. Feisty, annoying at times yes, pathetic no. You'll find your way again.' Gabby reached for her hand. 'I wish you'd told me. I'd have sent you the money to get you home.'

'Everything was fine at first. He was kind to me and were both happy. But then we discovered that the problems I had giving birth to Elodie, you remember those I'm sure, turned out to mean that I couldn't have any more children. It all went a bit sour after that and it was too late to change anything.'

'Did you have any friends you could talk to? Anybody who knew what was going on?'

Harriet shook her head. 'In the beginning but Todd slowly alienated my friends until they all dropped away.'

Gabby was quiet for a few moments as her long buried guilty feelings swamped her mind. Could she have done more to prevent Harriet going off the rails after her dad had died? Could she have prevented her falling pregnant? She'd done everything she could to support Harriet though, both before Elodie was born and afterwards. It was the time when Todd appeared on the scene that she felt the biggest guilt about. She should have tried harder, talked to Harriet more, told her she was making a mistake. Gabby pulled herself out of her reverie.

'How long have you been living in Bristol?'

'A couple of months. I kept trying to pluck up the courage to ring you, to come and see you but never quite found enough to actually do it. That's why I wrote the letter, it was easier. Your invitation to come to France for Christmas was quite unexpected. I wasn't sure about it. Still not, to be honest.'

'Why did you go to Bristol, why not come down to Devon where you belong?' Gabby asked. 'Did you feel you wouldn't be welcome because if you did, you are so wrong. I'd have welcomed you anytime with open arms.'

'I needed time to sort my head out, besides you might have been prepared to welcome me back but Elodie?' Harriet shrugged. 'I know she has never forgiven me for abandoning her and I'm not sure how I'll deal with that if she carries the grudge forever. Although she has every right to hate me for what I did.'

'I'm not sure grudge is the right word. She's never got over the hurt of her mummy leaving. Forever is the key word for both of you. As long as you are determined to try and have her in your life forever now and don't disappear again, given time she'll come round. You need to tell her the truth about the past and your hopes for the future. Elodie is not one to hate anybody.' Gabby stood up. 'Let's wander along the Promenade du Soleil. I want to show you something.'

'How are you for money?' Gabby asked as they began to walk.

'Todd left me everything, after regularly threatening me he was going to write a new Will and disinherit me. And there was a large insurance policy as well, so I'm actually quite well off. I'm only renting in Bristol until I decide where I'd like to live.'

The Promenade du Soleil was busy with families enjoying the

sunshine and they had to dodge around children on their, clearly new, presents of scooters and bikes from Christmas.

'We'll cross over here,' Gabby said decisively. 'It'll be quieter this way.'

Harriet shot her a look. 'What do you want to show me?'

'I told you there were a couple of reasons why I came to France this year. The main one is the house I grew up in and have owned now for ten years or so.'

As they walked through the quiet back streets of Juan-les-Pins, Gabby told Harriet about the house and the decision to not only keep it but also that she and Elodie were going to move to France and live in it.

'I can't tell you how excited Elodie is at the prospect. Right, it's just down here,' and they turned into the impasse.

Gabby took the keys out of her bag. 'Would you like to see around?'

'Of course.'

Harriet was quiet as Gabby showed her around the villa. 'You wouldn't find it difficult living back here? I know you loved Grandmère Odette but your father made life difficult for a few years for you, didn't he?'

Gabby nodded. 'He did. But the good memories of times in this house outweigh the negatives and having Elodie here will make a big difference.' A sudden idea popped into her mind that made her catch her breath. Was she being too impulsive? Was it too soon? What would Elodie say? She took a calming breath, hoping that what she was about to suggest was the right thing to do. 'How about you? There are three large bedrooms upstairs, one can be yours if you want it to be. For a long or short time. Would give you time to decide where and what you want to do.' Gabby said softly.

Harriet looked at her.

'How would Elodie feel about it? Have you mentioned this possibility to her?'

Gabby shook her head. 'No, it only just occurred to me as we wandered around. She might find it hard in the beginning, the three of us living together under one roof but it could be good. We'd all get to know each others' foibles first hand.' Gabby laughed.

'At least think about it. I find it ironic that you've returned to England and Elodie and I are planning to move here. Be good if you were to come too. All of us together on the same continent. Under the same roof, imagine. A new beginning for us all.'

Harriet gave her a smile. 'It probably wouldn't be easy but it would be good. I'll think about it but Elodie has to have the final say. If she's horrified at the thought of living in the same house as me, it's a no-go.'

Walking back to the apartment fifteen minutes later Gabby offered to buy Harriet lunch but she declined the offer.

'Another day would be lovely. I'm going to spend some time wandering around and getting a proper feel for the place.'

'You're welcome to join us in the apartment, you know, for the last few days, it sleeps six.'

'I think I need to meet up with Elodie first,' Harriet said. 'After that, we'll see.'

'I will see you on my birthday, won't I?' Gabby said. 'I'm sure Elodie will be planning something for the two of us. I'll ask her and text you the details. But come for lunch on the day anyway.'

'I'd love to see you on your birthday but I'm not sure Elodie will be keen.'

'It's my birthday and she always spoils me and makes sure I have a good day,' Gabby said confidently. 'Anyway, I hope to see you again before then.'

22

The two of them gave each other a spontaneous affectionate hug before they parted company. Gabby was in a daze as she began to make her way back to the apartment. It felt so good to be in touch with her daughter again but right now she was emotionally exhausted and feeling guilty. So guilty and sad that she hadn't been able to prevent Harriet being let down by the man she thought had loved her and for whom she'd left her family behind. She'd thought at the time that Harriet was making a mistake but Harriet insisted she knew what she was doing and didn't listen. The more Gabby had urged her to really think about what she was leaving behind, the more determined Harriet had become to go.

Elodie was in the kitchen preparing fromage and ham sandwiches for them both. She looked up at Gabby, a frown crossing her face. 'You all right?'

Gabby nodded automatically. 'Fine.'

'Did you get the coffee?'

Gabby looked at her blankly. 'Coffee, oh sorry, I forgot. I'll go this afternoon.'

'Okay. Are you sure you're all right?' Elodie stared at her.

'Just got something on my mind.' Gabby paused. 'I've been talking to Harriet.'

'Lucky you,' Elodie muttered, turning her attention back to the sandwiches.

Gabby sighed. 'She's not sure of the reception she'll receive from you. She hoped I would be pleased to see her, which I am, but it's you she's worried about.'

'Nothing for her to worry about because I'm not going to see her.'

'And that attitude is exactly what Harriet is afraid of. She wants to see you.' Gabby said. 'She's full of regret for the past and what she did. It's taken her two months to pluck up the courage to contact us.'

'Didn't rush then.'

'Elodie, please. None of this is easy but could you not try to meet her halfway and at least talk civilly to each other? For my sake if not your own. It might not seem like it to you, but I'm finding it difficult too. I remember how hard it was when she walked away from us.' Gabby was silent for a moment. 'There's nothing we can do to change the past but we can make a different future.'

Elodie's shoulders sagged but she didn't answer.

'I know you're probably arranging the usual special tea for the two of us on my birthday,' Gabby took a deep breath. 'I'd quite like it to be for the three of us this year.'

Gabby waited for a response but silence followed her words for several seconds. She sighed and was about to turn and walk away when Elodie spoke.

'Okay. It's your birthday. So for your sake I give in. Tell her to be here by four o'clock on the thirty-first and she can celebrate your birthday with us.' Elodie picked up the plate of sandwiches and made for the balcony with them.

'Thank you,' Gabby said. 'Glass of wine with lunch?' When Elodie nodded, Gabby poured two glasses and followed her out to the balcony.

The sandwiches were almost finished and the rosé drunk when Elodie looked at Gabby and broke the silence that surrounded them.

'So what did you talk about?'

'Harriet's life with Todd, which didn't turn out as she'd hoped,' Gabby said. 'But that's her story to tell you. When the two of you talk, I hope you will listen to her with an open mind. I don't expect you to forgive her for leaving in the first place, I'm having difficulty with that myself, but I hope you will be kind and try to forgive her when you learn the truth about why she didn't visit and rarely wrote.'

Elodie stayed silent as Gabby continued.

'One thing you need to know is that when we move here I've suggested she lives with us. There's plenty of room in No.5 and I feel it would help her to have family close for a while.'

'You didn't think to ask me how I felt about that?'

'It was an impulsive thing that I suddenly felt the need to suggest as I showed her No.5 this morning.'

'You've taken her to the villa?'

Gabby nodded.

Elodie gave a sigh as she fiddled with her empty wine glass. 'Do you think she will want to move in with us? I'm not sure I can...' her voice trailed away. 'It would certainly change things.'

Gabby shrugged. 'We'll have to wait and see what she decides. She did say she'd think about it but if you didn't like the idea it was a no-go.'

'Where is she staying at the moment?'

'One of the big modern hotels on the Boulevard Edouard Baudoin.'

'Not far away then.'

It was Gabby who broke the uncomfortable silence of several minutes that followed Elodie's last words.

'It would be good not to have an atmosphere between the three of us on my birthday. Would you meet her tomorrow? I'll come with you if you like.'

Elodie pulled a face. 'I'll think about it.'

And with that Gabby decided to let the matter drop. She'd have to have another try later.

* * *

After she left Gabby, Harriet caught the small shuttle bus into the centre of Antibes and treated herself to a panini and a glass of wine at one of the restaurant bars near the market. Surrounded by the animated buzz of several different languages as happy people laughed and joked with each other, Harriet sipped her drink, thinking about the welcome she'd received from Gabby. She remembered years ago wondering about her mother's amazing fortitude in the face of hurtful events with her generous and non-judgemental attitude towards people and happenings. A trait that Harriet had railed against as a teenager. Then, she'd never understood how her mother could be so gentle and forgiving. Today, she still couldn't understand totally but she appreciated and welcomed the attitude.

The waiter placed her freshly made jambon and fromage panini in front of with a smile. 'Merci.' she said.

How unexpected that her reunion with her mother had taken place in France, a place she remembered Gabby always refusing point blank to even talk about and had never once re-visited since leaving. Harriet had thrown several tantrums as a teenager wanting to have a holiday in the south of France. Something her mother had refused to even consider. Now, all these years later, she was planning on returning to live. Perhaps Gabby was harbouring more regrets about the past than she'd ever admit to.

As for the invitation to join Gabby and Elodie here in a new life, Harriet didn't know if she dared. The thought of them living together, finally bonding as the women of a three generation family, appealed but until she and Elodie had met face to face she wouldn't, couldn't, factor it into any plans she might make.

Gabby seemed confident that Elodie would come round to accepting her presence back in their lives, but Harriet wasn't so sure. Why should she? And if Elodie did accept her mother's presence in her life, would it be a willing acceptance, or merely an under sufferance one because she had no alternative?

Harriet finished her panini and drained her glass, resisting the urge to order another glass of wine. She heard her phone in her bag ping with an incoming text message. Pulling it out she glanced at the screen. Gabby:

Tea party 31st at the apartment four o'clock. Looking forward to seeing you then – if not before?

Harriet quickly answered:

Looking forward to it.

But ignored the question that followed it. With just one day before Gabby's birthday, her face to face meeting with Elodie needed to happen tomorrow. She was determined their first meeting after all this time would be a private one, just the two of them, with no-one, not even Gabby, witnessing their reunion.

Harriet put a twenty euro note under the empty wine glass and stood up. Time for a wander and to try and formulate some sort of Elodie action plan.

She'd dreamed for so long of living back in England, being in contact with Gabby and getting to know Elodie. There had been hours thinking about how things would settle themselves down. But moving to mainland Europe hadn't been in the plan. She couldn't help but feel that living in one foreign country in her lifetime was more than enough. Australia had been a culture shock in so many ways, but she'd been younger then, eager to experience everything that came her way, until the inevitable day of reckoning arrived and she realised she'd made the biggest mistake of her life. Would moving to France turn out to be the wrong decision for her too? Even if she would be living with at least one family member who truly cared about her.

Wandering past shop after shop Harriet tried to concentrate her thoughts on finding a birthday present for Gabby. The trouble was, she had no real idea of the things she liked these days. In the end she decided on a luxurious looking diary with a beautiful embossed leather cover and a colourful print at the beginning of each month. Standing by the counter, waiting to pay, Harriet noticed some pencils and pens packaged together with a sketch book, 'For the Artist in the family', and instinctively her hand went out and took one. So long since she'd owned a sketchbook, let alone drawn in one.

Harriet walked back to the hotel along the coast road of Cap d'Antibes, frequently stopping to admire the view. The snow-capped Alps behind her, the Esterel mountains in front, the sun dancing on the waves of the Mediterranean. It was a long walk and by the time she reached the boarded up Hôtel Le Provençal she'd reached a decision. If the meeting with Elodie went well, she'd seriously consider the idea of moving to France to be with her mother and daughter, but not necessarily living in the villa with them. She'd find her own place. If Elodie made it clear she didn't want her mother in her life, then she'd leave and make a new home for herself back in England and hope, given time, that Elodie would, if not forgive her, at the least accept her regrets and her heart-felt apologies for everything.

Now all she had to do was to try and meet up with Elodie before the birthday party. Back in her hotel room she picked up her iPad. She'd found Elodie's journalist contact e-mail address on-line weeks ago but had never found the courage to use it. The time had now come.

* * *

Gabby had left for the supermarket to buy the forgotten coffee and Elodie was proof-reading a feature on her laptop ready to send, when her e-mail programme pinged with an incoming message. Initially, she didn't recognise the address and was about to delete it as spam, then she took a second look and realised it was from her mother. Should she read it? If she deleted it without having read it she could maybe deny ever having received it. But Elodie knew there was no way she could do that and reluctantly clicked on the message.

Dear Elodie,

I know my turning up here was an unexpected and unwelcome inter-ruption to your Christmas and New Year holiday with Gabby and I also know you are angry and unhappy about my reappearance in your life. Please believe me when I say how much I regret my past actions, for not only the affect they had on you, but also on my mother. Gabby has graciously listened to me and I would like the chance to talk to you face to face and to offer you my apologies. I don't expect you to ever understand completely why I did what I did but I would hope that you have enough compassion to accept that sometimes we all make mistakes and do things we regret in life.

Please meet me, Elodie, and give me the opportunity to at least try to explain the dreadful wrong I did you twenty years ago. I am not asking for your forgiveness, now, or in the future. I just want you to know the truth about that time of my life.

I am very aware that it is impossible to erase my past actions but I sincerely hope that in the years to come there could be a time when we would at least acknowledge our relationship as mother and daughter.

I also long to know more about you and your dreams for the future. If you will allow me, I want to be in your life – as a friend if nothing more. With love,

Harriet.

Elodie slumped back against her chair as she finished reading the email and closed her eyes. Harriet had certainly got the 'angry and unhappy' bit right but hidden under that anger and bitterness there was also a raging deep desire to hear the truth about why Harriet had abandoned her. Something that Harriet did clearly regret.

A knock on the on the apartment door made her jump. Wanting to ignore it but knowing she couldn't in case it was Philippe with a message about the surprise party, Elodie opened it to see Gazz standing there with a bunch of mimosa which he held out to her.

'First of the season. Always make me feel winter is over down here when the mimosa starts to bloom.'

Elodie, struggling to push her thoughts about the email away and pull herself together, smiled at Gazz. 'Thank you. Come in. These are beautiful.'

'Are you okay?' Gazz asked, giving her a worried look. 'Not disturbing you, am I?'

Elodie shook her head. 'No, I've done most of the stuff I wanted to do today.'

'Does that mean I could entice you out for another ride on the scooter?'

Elodie pretended to think about it. 'D'you know, I think you could. Where would we go?'

'How about Cannes? Have you been?'

'No. That would be lovely,' Elodie said. 'Give me five minutes to change. And to write a note for Gabby.'

'I'll see you outside in ten,' Gazz said.

Elodie put the mimosa in water, left a note for Gabby, changed into her best jeans, grabbed her warm jacket and purse, and went downstairs.

Gazz handed her the helmet and helped her with the strap as before and within minutes she was sitting behind him, holding on tightly and they were off. They sped along the coast from Juan-les-Pins, through Golfe-Juan and were soon on the outskirts of Cannes. As they rounded a corner Elodie saw the Palm Beach complex on her left and then the Croisette took them all the way into Cannes.

They found a parking space by the Carlton Hotel and Gazz took her hand as they crossed the road to walk along the pedestrian part of the Croisette towards the Palais des Festivals.

'Want to do the tourist thing and take a selfie of us on the steps?' Gazz said.

'Yes.' Laughing, they stood halfway up the famous steps and with an arm around her shoulders pulling her close, Gazz took a photo with his phone.

As they walked slowly away from the Palais des Festivals, Gazz took her hand again. Fleetingly, Elodie wondered whether she should gently withdraw it on account of Fiona being his girl-friend, before remembering how Gazz had said on Boxing Day that his new business was nothing to do with Fiona. If they were close, surely he would have taken Fiona's concerns into account. Gazz was a Frenchman who oozed charm but Elodie was 99 per cent certain that he wasn't the type to cheat on his girlfriend.

'I'm sorry Granddad Philly upset you the other evening. He was mortified he'd made you cry.' Gazz said, breaking the silence that had grown up between them.

'I'd hoped neither of you had noticed that,' Elodie said. 'Tell Philippe not to worry. It's not the first time I've shed tears over my mother and I'm not expecting it to be the last.'

'That's sad,' Gazz said, squeezing her hand. Elodie was grateful when he didn't say anything else and they continued to walk in silence. The afternoon light was fading and the Christmas decorations were coming on and Elodie spun around trying to take them all in, causing a laughing Gazz to spin with her as he wouldn't let go of her hand.

'I thought the lights in Antibes were brilliant and these are not better but brilliant in a different way. And the trees are beau-tiful. Isn't it strange how everyone is desperate to see the lights before Christmas and forgets they're still here to be enjoyed for a few weeks afterwards.'

There were chalets further along the quay and Elodie gave Gazz's hand a quick tug as they passed the entrance to the Christmas village.

'Can we have a quick look please? I haven't bought anything yet for Gabby's birthday. I might be inspired.'

The chalets, like those in the Antibes Christmas market, were selling a vast selection of things. Jewellery, clothes, food, paint-ings, ornaments, books, toys and cakes. Elodie came to a sudden stop in front of the cake stand.

'I've forgotten about a cake for Gabby. I'll have to go to the patisserie tomorrow morning and hope I have time to order one.'

Gazz groaned. 'I'm sorry. I'd forgotten I was instructed to tell you that Granddad Philly, to quote him, "has the cake in hand". And I can tell you, he makes the best cakes.'

'Really? That is so lovely of him to take the trouble to make a cake for someone he barely knows.'

'I think he plans on getting to know Gabriella better when you're living here,' Gazz said quietly.

Leaving the Christmas market, they walked alongside the harbour admiring the boats before reluctantly turning to retrace their steps to the scooter. Walking back along the Croisette, hand in hand with Gazz, Elodie took a deep breath. She couldn't talk to her grandmother about how she felt about Harriet without upsetting her but she definitely wanted to talk to someone and she knew instinctively that Gazz would listen without judgement.

Harriet's e-mail flashed into her guilty mind. She knew she should have replied to it before she came out with Gazz.

'Can I talk to you about my mother? Ask your advice?' she asked quietly.

'Ask away,' Gazz said.

'Gabby wants me to meet up with Harriet before her birthday because she has invited her to the birthday tea. She's also invited her to live with us once we move over here. And now Harriet has e-mailed me, asking to meet so we can get to know each other and she can explain the whys and wherefores of what she did. Suddenly I feel I'm being coerced into a situation I don't want to be in. Things are changing too fast.'

She snuffled and tried to stop the tears from starting. 'I'm sorry, I didn't mean for the waterworks to start again,' and she searched in her pocket for a tissue to wipe her face with.

Gazz led her over to a seat under a large tree and as they both sat down, he put his arm around her and held her close.

'I know everyone will see me as some kind of hard bitch if I don't agree to meet her, listen to what she has to say. But to have her appear back in my life without any real warning has left me reeling and I honestly do not know what to do.'

'First, nobody will think you're any kind of bitch. From the little I've seen of Gabby I don't think she'd coerce you into anything. She's been on your side ever since your mother left. But I do think she wants her daughter back in her life and the rift between the three of you healed.'

'All the time I was growing up, Gabby kept her feelings about Harriet to herself. She never once bad-mouthed her. It wasn't until I was oh, sixteen or seventeen I suppose, that I realised how hurt Gabby had been when she left us,' Elodie said. 'So deep down I know I should at least try to get on with my mother for Gabby's sake.'

Gazz nodded. 'For your sake too. I think you'll regret it if you don't. Meet her as Gabby wants you to, before the birthday tea, so that you can both be there for Gabby. We all make mistakes, do things we regret. The important thing is that we learn from them. Meet her as the adult you are now and not the child she left behind. New Year is a good time to start to heal festering wounds. And the birthday party will hopefully give you the impetus to putting your mother's past behaviour behind you.'

Elodie leaned in against him. 'Thank you. I shall pull on my big girl pants and contact her.'

Gazz looked at her. 'Big girl pants?'

Elodie laughed at the look on his face. 'It's an English expression – supposed to make you feel brave and like Wonder Woman,' Elodie clenched her fist and flexed her arm.

'All will be well, you'll see,' Gazz said. 'You're living your own life, she's living hers. It doesn't sound as if she plans on trying to interfere in yours, although once she's settled in, if she's anything like my maman, that might change.

'Your mum is lovely.'

'She likes you too.' Gazz said. 'As do I,' he added quietly. 'A lot.' And he pulled her closer into a tight hug.

Elodie pushed a fleeting thought of Fiona away. She'd talk to Gazz later. Find out exactly how close he and Fiona were and if they were more than friends, then she'd step back. But right now, she needed this hug.

There is nothing in the world as irresistibly contagious as laughter or good humour.

— CHARLES DICKENS. A CHRISTMAS CAROL.

23

The next morning, Elodie did the croissant run as usual and joined Gabby on the balcony for breakfast.

'Any plans for today?' Gabby asked.

'None that I can tell you about,' Elodie teased. 'You?'

'I thought I'd see if Harriet would like to come for lunch here today with us,' Gabby said with a questioning look on her face.

Elodie sighed. 'Gabby, please don't push so hard. I will talk to her when I'm ready, I promise. If it doesn't happen before the tea party tomorrow afternoon, I also promise not to make an atmosphere or spoil things. Okay?'

Gabby nodded. 'I'm sorry, I guess I'm pushing too hard. It's just,' she gave a deep sigh. 'I so want you and her to be reconciled.'

'I know you do.' Elodie gave her grandmother a compassionate look. 'But you trying to engineer things won't help. You must see that.'

'I do but now Harriet is back I want things to be good between us all as soon as possible.'

'And that is something I really do not understand. Why or

how you are able to be so welcoming to her after the way she left you literally holding the baby?'

Gabby twisted her bottom lip and swallowed a sigh before replying. 'Because I remember the years before she left us. Before your granddad died and Harriet lost her way. She had her future all mapped out – art college and a creative career, before meeting someone, getting married and having a family. Instead, she,' Gabby shrugged, her eyes wet. 'I feel I let her down. That's why I want to help her. I want her to find a better future than her past has been. Is that so wrong of me?'

Elodie shook her head and stood up to begin clearing the breakfast things. 'No, it's not wrong. Have lunch with her if that's what you want. The two of you can talk about the past – you don't need me around for that.'

After placing the dirty dishes in the dishwasher, she grabbed her jacket and purse. 'Right now, I'm going for a walk. I'll see you later.'

After Elodie left, Gabby went into her bedroom and began to methodically tidy clothes that didn't need tidying. It was her hands and mind that needed to be kept busy to stop her thinking about the distance between the two people she loved the most and whom she desperately wanted to be reconciled.

Elodie made her way down to the boulevard Édouard Baudoin wondering which of the modern hotels Harriet was staying in. Only one way to find out and that was to ask.

The receptionist in the first hotel gave the computer screen a quick glance when Elodie asked if a Madame Rogers was booked in and shook his head. The woman behind the reception desk in the second hotel gave a friendly smile as Elodie asked her the same question.

'Yes. She, Madame Rogers, stays here.'

Elodie heaved a sigh of relief. 'Great. Is it possible you can tell me her room number, s'il vous plait? Or maybe buzz her to tell her she has a visitor?'

The receptionist looked at her. 'Is she expecting you?'

'No. Not exactly, but she will be pleased to see me.'

'Are you a relative?'

Elodie nodded. 'Yes. This is a surprise visit.' She hesitated. 'She's my mother. So?'

'Madam Rogers, she stays here but she is not here at the moment.'

Elodie's shoulders sagged. She'd hoped to be early enough to catch Harriet before she left to pursue any plans she'd made for the day.

'No, she is out there on the beach.' And the receptionist pointed outside.

'Oh. Okay, thank you.' And Elodie wheeled around and left the hotel. Crossing the road to the beach she hoped there wouldn't be too many single women on the beach at this hour and that she'd be able to recognise her mother if there were.

Once on the beach itself Elodie scanned it in both directions. No single figures of either sex in sight except for one near the stone jetty with its newly erected jet ski hire sign. If that figure was Gazz he might have seen her mother, she started to walk towards the jetty but the closer she got she could tell that it was neither her mother or Gazz. Disappointed, she turned away and began to make for the top of the beach. It was then she saw the woman sitting alone on one of the boulevard benches and concentrating intently on something in her hand.

Elodie slowed her pace and walked along the beach for

several metres or so before heading back up towards the boulevard and making her way closer to the bench. She stopped nearby and stared. Was it Harriet? She had no real way of knowing but instinct told her that it was her mother sitting there concentrating on a sketch book. The woman, sensing her presence, glanced up and Elodie froze. There was no doubting that this was her mother. It was like looking at Gabby's face and into the same eyes.

Harriet closed the sketch book and patted the seat. 'Would you like to sit with me?'

Elodie gave a mute nod and moved to sit next to her. 'You look just like Gabby.'

'She's my mother, so that is inevitable, I suppose,' Harriet said. 'And I don't want to worry you but you'll probably end up looking like me.'

The two of them sat in silence for several moments, both staring out at the sea, both wondering how to start the conversation they were aware they needed and one that had to happen.

'Did you get my email?' Harriet asked.

Elodie nodded. 'Why did you leave? Was it anything to do with me? You didn't love me?'

Harriet looked at her, shocked, but didn't answer immediately. A lengthy silence had descended again before she took a deep breath. 'Elodie, you have to believe me when I say it was absolutely nothing to do with you. I loved you more than I believed it possible to love anyone. As to why I left, that's a question I've asked myself so many times down the years and the honest answer is, I left because I was stupid. It was the biggest mistake of my life. I can try to blame it on the fact that I went off the rails when my dad died, I missed him so much. Becoming a single mother meant all my dreams of going to art college vanished. However much Gabby supported me and she did, I knew it was impossible. When Todd came along, a suave successful man, promising to take care of me, I couldn't resist. Gabby tried talking to me, telling me he was too old for me, that she had doubts about him but I shrugged it all off, convinced she was wrong. Convinced he was the man for me.' Harriet fell silent again for a moment.

'Even when he said he wanted to marry me but didn't want the responsibility of you, I still didn't break off the relationship, which I should have done. No man who has any sense of decency would wilfully separate a mother from her young child, would they? Or drag them halfway across the world to Australia for a new life.' She glanced at Elodie who shrugged. 'I knew Gabby would love you and look after you. But I didn't know then that Todd was already lying to me when he promised I'd be able to come back regularly, stay in your life. I know now he had no intention of allowing that to happen.'

'So, why didn't you leave him? Come back home?'

'Everything was okay for a couple of years. Although every time I wanted to come back and see you Todd always had a business reason for why it wasn't convenient for him but he always promised we'd go soon. He didn't want me to work so I didn't have any money of my own. It took a few years before I fully realised how he controlled every aspect of my life – and how I'd adapted and changed myself to fit in with what he wanted. By then, of course, it was too late to escape.'

'Why? Elodie demanded.

'Because I lived in a foreign country that had never really become home, I had no friends to turn to, no money and zero confidence that I could survive on my own.' Harriet said quietly. 'You have no idea what it's like to be so dependent on one person. Under their control.' Harriet shivered. 'After Todd's death I managed to hold everything together until the funeral but then I went completely to pieces.' She paused and stared out at the sea for a moment.

'It was the solicitor handling the legal stuff who said something that finally got through to me. I'd signed the last of the papers and he was placing them all in a folder when he said, now that you are a free woman, Harriet, why don't you return to England? I think you'd be a happier woman there. It was as if he'd given me permission to leave. He was so kind when I burst into tears at the idea.'

'Did he know about Todd's treatment of you?'

'I think he'd guessed,' Harriet admitted. 'I did try to talk to him once at some social do, on behalf of a friend, you know?' She gave Elodie a wry smile. 'He was Todd's lawyer after all and naively I didn't want him thinking it was me I was talking about. But I guess he suspected.'

'So you're back in Europe for good?'

'Yes.'

'Gabby is thrilled that you're back.'

'How about you?' Harriet said.

'Depends.'

'On what?'

'How much of a mother you plan on being.'

'I haven't planned on being anything,' Harriet said softly. 'But I would like to get to know you as a person and to be in your life if you'll let me.' She took a battered leather wallet out of her jacket pocket. 'I know I was wrong to leave you and I'll never stop regretting that but I never forgot about you.' Harriet opened the wallet and carefully took out a piece of folded sketch paper scotch taped together on the reverse. 'It's been everywhere with me all the time I've been away.' She handed it to Elodie.

Gently unfolding it, Elodie stared at the pen and ink drawing. The two figures she saw were instantly recognisable. Gabby, sitting in her chair by the fire in their sitting room at home, with Elodie on her lap, as she read her a story.

'Gabby told me this morning you were planning to go to art college,' she said, folding the paper carefully and handing back. 'You should have gone. You're good.'

Harriet shrugged. 'Maybe I was an artist once, not now. Although I do have a small urge to maybe try again.' She put the wallet back in her pocket. 'Gabby has invited me to her birthday tea at the apartment tomorrow, are you happy that I come?'

Elodie shrugged nonchalantly. 'Gabby wants you there so you should come but it's not at the apartment. Philippe helped me with organising tea at a restaurant Gabby likes, as a surprise. You can either meet us at the restaurant at four o'clock or come to the apartment a little earlier and walk there with us.'

'I'll meet you there if you give me the details,' Harriet said.

'It's not far from the apartment,' and Elodie fished in her pocket for the card Philippe had given her. 'Here you go. I'll see you there then.'

'Would you like to come back to the hotel for a coffee now?' Harriet said. 'You know a little bit more about me, I'd like to get to know you a bit better.

Elodie shook her head and stood up. 'I'm sorry. I've a few things I need to do this morning. See you tomorrow.' She started to walk away before turning to look at Harriet. 'I think Gabby would like to have lunch with you today though.' She gave Harriet a half smile before turning away again.

Harriet nodded and watched her as she walked away. Tentative olive branches seemed to have been offered on both sides but it was going to take time for relations to settle down and become easier between them. She realised Elodie had to learn to trust her, to accept that she wasn't going to disappear again. Harriet knew there was no way she could ever do that a second time to either

her daughter or her mother but it was going to take time to convince Elodie, in particular, of that. What was the old saying? Once bitten twice shy. She wouldn't make the same mistake again.

Sighing, Harriet opened the sketch pad, her fingers itching to capture an image of her grownup daughter's face. The pencil moved across the page hesitantly at first but soon there were strong lines appearing on the paper and, as she became more confident, Elodie's face with the small smile she'd given her as she left, materialised on the page.

24

After leaving Harriet, Elodie didn't feel like going straight back to the apartment so instead she walked around the narrow streets behind the Promenade du Soleil thinking about Harriet and how open she'd been talking about the biggest mistake of her life. Elodie wished she'd accepted the offer of coffee in the hotel. At the very least she could have finally asked Harriet about her father: what was he like, why had he never figured in her life? Why wasn't his name on her birth certificate? Harriet clearly wanted to learn a few things about Elodie but there was no way she was ready for an intimate conversation with her mother.

Besides, down the years, Gabby would have given her the highlights of school, college and work, so Harriet knew a lot about her already. Whereas she barely knew anything about Harriet because she'd refused to listen when Gabby tried to talk to her about her mother. The more personal stuff, like the anger she'd felt for years with Harriet when she'd realised that her mother had simply walked away from her, was bubbling away under the surface and it wouldn't take much for it to break through. Besides, she'd promised Gabby there wouldn't be an atmosphere at the tea party and she intended to keep that promise however much she felt the need to confront Harriet about her unkind and devastating behaviour all those years ago. Deep down, she was already beginning to acknowledge how much Harriet herself had suffered after she'd taken the decision to leave.

Four days after Christmas and many of the shop windows still had their festive decorations in place although a couple had changed the 'Joyous Noël' banner for a 'Bonne Année' one. Elodie stopped in front of one with hats, handbags, belts and scarves on show. She still had to find a birthday present for Gabby. Would she like a new handbag? Or that creamy coloured silk scarf with the bird of paradise pattern which was beautiful. Elodie sighed. Neither seemed special enough for Gabby's seventieth birthday. Although the silk scarf was rather lovely. If she couldn't find anything else she'd come back later and buy it, she decided.

Elodie wandered on, lost in thought, barely noticing where she was going and found herself standing by an archway over a small opening with the words 'Brocante/Antiquities' painted on a wooden sign. She walked under the archway and found herself on a gravel path leading towards a wooden building that looked to be part house, part shop. An ancient bicycle painted blue and yellow, its wicker basket holding pots of early sweet smelling pink hyacinths, was propped against the wall near the open shop door.

Walking inside, Elodie stopped and looked around. Everything was a jumble and yet there was a detectable semblance of order. Furniture including tables, chairs, bureaus, armoires and bookcases were to one side. China, glasses, ornaments and pictures were in the middle and down the other side were curtains, cushions, fabrics, a rail of clothes, a few books and cuddly toys. Narrow walkways led the way between everything.

A woman sitting at a table near the entrance glanced up as Elodie entered.

'Bonjour, mademoiselle.' But she made no attempt to ask if Elodie was looking for something in particular or to offer assistance. Elodie returned the greeting and began to make her way, carefully, around. Some of the furniture was definitely in the antique league but most of it was pretty ordinary. Good stuff for up cycling though, when they moved into No.5. Edging past a large table piled high with china and ornaments, a flash of yellow caught Elodie's eye and she stepped closer to take a look. It was a large rectangular dish with small grooves moulded in the corner edges at right angles to each of the four sides. But it was the fine blue writing painted across the face of the dish that made Elodie catch her breath. Le Hôtel de Provençal. She picked the dish up and walked to the woman to ask the price. Not that she needed to know the price, she was buying it anyway.

'Forty euros, s'il vous plait.'

Elodie placed the dish on the table to retrieve her purse from her bag and handed over the money. 'It's my grandmother's seventieth birthday demain. She's going to adore this as a fun cadeau. She used to work in that hotel years ago.' She smiled at the woman, realising she was gabbling away in a mixture of English with the odd French word she could remember thrown in and the poor woman probably didn't understand any of it.

The woman paused from putting the dish in a bag and gave Elodie a quick look. 'I also put my carte de business in the bag, in case you have need to contact me. Or want to buy something else.'

'I'll definitely be back. We're moving to Juan-les-Pins in the New Year. I'll bring Gabby, that's my grandmother, next time too.'

The woman smiled as she handed the bag over. 'Wish your grandmère Happy Birthday from me.'

'Merci beaucoup.' And, clutching the bag, Elodie wandered back out into the street again. This time she made a note of exactly where she was so that she could find the place again when they moved over. She found her way back to the shop with the handbags and hats and went in and bought the silk scarf for Gabby. She nodded when the assistant asked if it was a gift and the scarf was swiftly placed in a box and wrapped in some pretty paper and tied with a ribbon bow.

When she got back to the apartment Gabby was in the sitting room, flipping through one of the magazines they'd bought before Christmas.

'I was hoping you'd be back soon. Harriet has invited me to lunch with her. Are you sure you won't join us?'

Elodie shook her head. 'Did she tell you that we met up this morning on the beach?'

A wide smile spread across Gabby's face. 'You did? No, she didn't say anything. How, how did the two of you get on?'

'We talked a bit about her life. She admitted that leaving us was the biggest mistake of her life. One that she will regret forever.'

'Did you talk to her? About how you feel?'

Elodie shook her head. 'It's too soon.'

'Well, it's a start, thank you, Elodie.'

25

New Year Eve was promising to be a beautiful sunny day to celebrate Gabby's special birthday. Elodie was busy cooking Gabby's favourite birthday breakfast, pancakes with cream and maple syrup, the next morning when Gabby appeared in the kitchen.

'Happy Birthday, Gabby,' Elodie said, leaving the stove long enough to give her a hug. 'Everything is out on the balcony, if you'd like to take the coffee out, I'll bring the pancakes, I'm just finishing the last one,' and she turned it out on top of the others.

Elodie carried the dish of pancakes out to the balcony. 'I thought as we're in France I'd do my version of Crêpes Suzette,' she said, placing the dish on the table. She picked up a miniature bottle of Cointreau and poured it carefully over the hot pancakes before striking a match and holding the flame over the plate to set the alcohol alight.

'I know they should really be flambeéd in the pan but I didn't want to do it in the kitchen. Just in case.'

'They smell delicious,' Gabby said, sniffing appreciatively.

Once the pancakes had been devoured and they were on their

second cups of coffee, Gabby looked at the two gifts. 'Can I open them now?'

Elodie pushed the flat boxed one across. 'Open this one first. The other one is just something I found and thought you'd like.'

Gabby was delighted with the silk scarf. 'Beautiful. I think it's going to become one of my favourites,' she said, draping it around her neck. Reaching for the other parcel she looked at Elodie. 'This feels heavy.'

Elodie nodded, watching for her reaction, hoping the memories it was sure to stir would be good ones. Gabby gave a gasp as she took the dish out of the bag.

'I never thought to see one of these again,' she said, placing it on the table, a happy smile on her face.

'You like it? I thought you could use it for keys and things on the dresser we are going to have in the kitchen of No.5.'

'We're having a dresser?'

'Definitely,' Elodie said. 'It's crying out for one. As for the dish, I can imagine it being useful for lots of things but please, do you know what the grooves in the edges are for?'

Gabby looked at her with disbelief. 'You really don't know?' She laughed. 'Times have changed. It's an ashtray for cigarettes. There were lots of them throughout the hotel. Everybody smoked in those days, you could rest your lit cigarette down in the groove. Where did you find it?'

'The most amazing second hand place. I was just wandering around and there it was, through an archway. Brocante/Antiquities. It's a real Aladdin's Cave off one of the back streets in Juan. I'm pretty certain I can find it again but I have the address anyway.' Elodie jumped up and fetched the business card the lady had put in the bag from her bedroom.

'Here's the address. The lady who sold it to me was really nice. Said to wish you a happy birthday when I told her the dish was a present for my grandmother. The place looked as if it had been there forever. Could even have been there when you lived here.'

Gabby took the card and gave a smile. 'It was. Colette's family ran it.' She looked at the card again. 'Different name now, though. They must have sold the place on. Shame.' She gave the dish a stroke. 'I love it. A real piece of history that means something to me. Thank you.'

'So what would you like to do today?' Elodie smiled at her grandmother. There was a pause before Gabby answered her.

'I plan on spending the day with the two people who mean the most to me, you and Harriet, so I've asked her to join us for the day, not just for tea this afternoon.' She gave Elodie an anxious look. 'You've broken the ice by meeting her yesterday, today can be another step forward, a bit more glue to stick us together properly.'

Elodie smothered a sigh, hoping her grandmother didn't notice, and plastered a smile on her face. The last thing she wanted was to spend so much time with Harriet but Gabby was clearly intent on them both forging a new bond with her now that she was here. 'Okay. What time are we all meeting up?'

'Harriet is coming here at about ten o'clock. I thought I'd run down to the patisserie and get some cream cakes,' Gabby said.

'I'll go,' Elodie said. 'I can see today is going to be all about eating and drinking and I'm going to need all the exercise I can get.'

Guiltily, Elodie deliberately timed going out for the cakes so that she would miss Harriet's arrival at the apartment.

When she got back she quickly put several cream cakes on a plate and carried them out to the balcony where she could hear Gabby and Harriet chatting.

'Hi,' she said, acknowledging Harriet's presence with a quick look as she placed the plate on the table. 'Coffee or pink champagne? I put a bottle in the fridge yesterday to chill. Gabby?'

'Champagne sounds wonderful but I think maybe coffee. Save the champagne for afternoon tea.' Gabby looked at her. 'You haven't told me the plans for this afternoon yet?'

'No, I haven't and I'm not going to – it's a surprise. You'll have to be patient and wait and see.'

'Coffee it is. Gabby and I take it black, no sugar. How about you?' Elodie asked Harriet as she turned to go to the kitchen.

'Splash of milk, no sugar, please.'

Standing in the kitchen waiting for the coffee to brew and listening to Gabby laughing at something Harriet had said, Elodie realised just how much her grandmother was loving having her daughter back in her life. When she took the coffees out to the balcony, Gabby was showing Harriet the ashtray and her new scarf. After admiring them, Harriet reached into the bag at her feet and handed her mother a parcel and an envelope. 'Happy Birthday, Mum.' And she leant forward and kissed her on the cheek.

Gabby opened the parcel and took out the embossed leather diary and planner. 'I didn't know what to get you but I thought as you're going to have a lot to plan and organise next year this might be useful.' Harriet said.

'It will, thank you,' Gabby said. 'I love how the monthly photos mark the changing seasons throughout the year.' She put the diary down and picked up the envelope and pulled out a handmade card.

'Oh, Harry,' she said, using the long ago pet name for her daughter. 'This is lovely. Thank you.' She brushed away a tear. 'I shall find a frame for it and hang it in my bedroom. Elodie, look, see what your talented mother has made,' and she handed the card across to her.

Harriet had sketched a three generation portrait of them all sitting on a bench by the pool in No.5. Elodie stared at the picture with its strange over print of faint lines, some of which were broken. What on earth? And then she realised, when she saw the small spider drawn in the left hand corner, it was a symbolic, intricate lace-like cobweb linking the three of them together, despite their fractured lives down the years. Inside Harriet had written 'Happy Birthday and Happy New Year. All my love Harriet.'

Elodie looked at her mother. 'Gabby is right, you are talented. Why did you really give it up?'

'I always used to carry a sketch book around with me, to catch fleeting ideas and impressions, remember, Mum?' Harriet asked, glancing at her mother. Gabby nodded.

'Todd didn't like me doing that. He said I was bringing unnecessary attention to myself by drawing in public. Besides, I'd never be more than an amateur, and not a good one at that, so why bother? My mistake, again, was that I allowed him to say those things and I believed him.'

'Well, we both think you're extremely talented and it's never too late to follow your dreams,' Gabby said. 'In fact, it will be a punishable offence if you fail to utilise your gift.'

Harriet shook her head. 'Maybe. I did enjoy doing your card.'

'Well, I warn you, when we're all living in No.5 I shall be merciless in urging you to draw,' Gabby said.

'Hang on. I haven't said I am coming to live with you,' Harriet said. 'I'm not at all sure that the three of us living together is that good an idea.'

Elodie kept the thought, that makes two of us then, to herself.

There was a pause. 'We could at least give it a try, couldn't we?' Gabby asked.

Harriet shook her head. 'I don't know. We've been apart for so long and—'

'And that's precisely why we need to live together and get to know each other as a family.' Gabby interrupted firmly.

Elodie looked at the two of them. 'Listening to the two of you it sounds as if you've slipped back into the perfect mother and daughter arguing mode already.' Even to her own ears she sounded petulant.

Crossly, she started to clear the cups and plates away. Given that Harriet had left her for so many years what were the chances that the two of them would ever have the kind of mother daughter relationship that should have developed between them naturally?

And more to the point, did she actually want one?

26

The three of them decided that they needed to work off at least some of the calories of the cream cakes before lunch and Gabby suggested walking into Antibes. 'We can have a wander around the old town followed by a visit to a special museum I want to show you.'

'You'll love it, I promise you,' Gabby said, sensing their joint hesitation over the museum suggestion. 'It's a fun place. And we can have lunch close by.'

An hour later they were approaching the ancient ramparts in Antibes when Gabby led them down a narrow street lined with ancient terraced cottages. Harriet took out her phone and started to take photos as they walked. Old wooden doors with crackled faded paint and fancy metal latches, windows with weathered shutters half open and an ancient olive tree with the roots of its gnarled trunk disappearing under the cracked tarmac. Perhaps when she was more settled she'd take inspiration from them for a painting.

Their meandering finally led them to the bustling market and they joined the slowly moving crowd to walk its length. Even in mid winter, the fruit and vegetable stands were colourful with a variety of peppers and tomatoes and oranges and lemons from Corsica alongside the more mundane lettuces and potatoes. Elodie longed to taste some of the cheeses on the fromage stall but didn't like to sample without buying. She promised herself she'd be a regular customer when she lived down here.

The narrow street they turned into as they left the market was lined with shops and several art galleries displaying paintings and sculptures.

'Antibes is a real arty town, isn't it?' Harriet said.

'Yes,' Gabby answered. 'You're going to fit right in here.' She gave her daughter a cheeky smile and moved away before Harriet could respond.

'Are we stopping for lunch soon? Seeing the food in the market and all our walking has made me hungry,' Elodie asked.

'We're five minutes away from the restaurant, it's down here,' and Gabby led the way into Place Nationale. 'I wanted to show you the Peynet and Cartoon Museum first but it's probably closed for lunch now, we'll visit this afternoon,' and she walked on past the bandstand to one of the restaurants in the corner of the square.

'Is that Raymond Peynet, the man who famously drew 'Amoureux' – the poet and his lover – back in the forties?' Harriet asked. 'He had such a recognisable style – simple lines and colouring that instantly draws one into the story of the picture.'

'Yes, that's him,' Gabby said.

They decided to sit at an outside table for lunch and were soon tucking into the plat du jour, a warming and filling cassoulet, washed down by a bottle of the house red wine which they shared between them. The waiter taking their empty plates away asked if they would like a dessert, Gabby looked at Elodie.

'Will there be cake for tea? If there is, I won't have a dessert.

Only I haven't seen any signs in the apartment of birthday cake preparations.'

'Of course there will be cake for tea as well as the champagne,' Elodie said. 'When have I ever not got a cake for your birthday? Though I admit that this year I haven't made it. I have to collect it later, okay? And don't worry, I'm all organised for a proper birthday tea later.'

Elodie and Harriet also decided to forego dessert and Gabby asked for the bill, which Harriet quickly intercepted. 'I think it's about time I bought you a birthday lunch, so no arguing.'

Together they made their way over to the museum only to be disappointed by the notice at the entrance:

Closed until January 2nd

'I guess it goes on the To Do list for when we live here, something to look forward to. Now,' Elodie said. 'Shall we get the shuttle bus back or walk?'

'Shuttle bus,' Gabby and Harriet said in unison.

Half an hour later they were back at the apartment. Gabby went to her room saying she was going to have a short nap to boost her strength for the rest of the day. 'And to let you do whatever you have to do before four o'clock.'

Harriet and Elodie looked at each other as the bedroom door closed. 'I could go back to the hotel for a bit,' Harriet said, glancing at her watch. 'Although it hardly seems worth it as it's three o'clock now.'

'No point,' Elodie agreed. 'Cup of tea?'

Harriet nodded and followed her into the kitchen. 'While we're on our own, this tea party. I'd like to pay for it.'

Elodie shook her head. 'Thank you, but there's no need. I have it covered.'

'I'm sure you do but I'd really like to do something to begin to feel I'm part of the family again now that I'm back. At the very least could we go halves?'

Elodie was silent for several seconds before giving a brief nod. 'Okay. we'll divide it between us. I have no idea how much it's going to be as Philippe booked the restaurant but it won't be as expensive as the Belles Rives.' She threw a couple of teabags in the pot as the kettle boiled and made the tea. 'Balcony or sitting room?'

'Balcony. This is a lovely apartment.'

'We were so lucky to find it,' Elodie said, pouring the tea. 'It was literally the only place with the availability we needed.'

Sitting out on the balcony with its glimpse of the sea beyond La Pinède, Harriet hesitated as she looked at her daughter, before voicing her concern.

'Are you able yet to tell me how you truly feel about the possibility of me moving in with you and Gabby. I know she dreams of the three of us living under the same roof but what about you? How do you feel?'

Elodie sipped her tea. 'I'm not sure to be honest. The relationship Gabby and I have has evolved into something more than grandmother and granddaughter while it's been just the two of us. You coming back has already changed things. Moving in and living with us is sure to change the dynamics even more. But maybe that would be a good thing? I don't know.' She hesitated. 'What I do know though, is that Gabby would be totally devastated if you leave again, whether you move into No.5 with us or not.'

Harriet looked at her steadily. 'I promise I have absolutely no intention of leaving either of you again but is living 'en famille' something we should jump into without getting to know each other again first, or should we wait.' She shrugged.

'I know Gabby wouldn't be happy moving from Devon and leaving you in the UK on your own,' Elodie said. 'In fact, she'd probably change her mind about coming to France, and let the house out again.' Elodie looked at her mother. 'So, we should probably go for you moving in with us and letting things take their course because I think Gabby really wants to spend the rest of her life here in the town where she was born and grew up. And who are we to deny her that?'

Harriet nodded thoughtfully. 'It's going to take several weeks to organise the move anyway so hopefully you and I will at least know each other better by then – we might even be friends,' she added quietly.

'You never know.' Elodie gave Harriet a half smile as she stood up. 'Gabby will be up soon. We'll need to get a move on.'

As if on cue, Gabby appeared looking happy and refreshed with the bird of paradise scarf around her neck. 'Nearly four o'clock – time for tea?'

'Yes,' Elodie said. 'First though, we need to go and collect the cake.'

Gabby looked surprised. 'We're all going for that?'

'Yep, afraid so. Another walk.'

Leaving the apartment block, the three of them walked arm in arm with Gabby in the middle. It was only a minute or two before Gabby spoke.

'We're not collecting a cake, are we? Which restaurant are you taking me to?'

'You'll see, we're nearly there,' Elodie said. 'I'm sorry it's not the Belles Rives but...' she shrugged.

Minutes later, Gabby recognised the restaurant where Philippe had taken her and looked at Elodie. 'Here?'

Elodie nodded as Harriet opened the door and they both

ushered her in to a rousing chorus of 'Happy Birthday' led by Philippe.

27

As she stood there listening to her new friends singing, Gabby clapped her hands in delight. A waiter appeared at her side with a tray of sparkling pink champagne and handed her a glass. 'Merci,' she said, in a daze from the surprise of it all. She registered the 'Happy 70th Birthday' banner strung across one of the restaurant walls, with bunches of balloons at either end, the tea party table set with beautiful china crockery, where another waiter was busy placing plates of sandwiches and a three-tiered cake stand filled with cakes of all descriptions. She'd guessed that Elodie was up to something from the lack of preparations in the apartment but hadn't expected it to involve Philippe and his family.

'What a wonderful surprise. Thank you all so much.' Gabby said.

Philippe walked forward to greet Harriet, his hand held out. 'Harriet, it's a pleasure to meet you. This rabble is my family,' and he quickly introduced her to them before turning back to Gabby. Taking her by the hand, he led her to the seat at the head of the party table.

'This all looks amazing,' Gabby said, looking at the food.

Everyone was soon chatting happily away as they tucked into the food and a waiter kept their glasses filled with champagne. Gabby turned to Philippe who was on her right.

'Thank you for helping Elodie to arrange this. It's absolutely perfect.'

Philippe glanced at her champagne glass, still with a respectable amount of pink liquid, before looking at the waiter who was hovering and giving him an almost imperceptible nod.

'I saw that nod,' Gabby whispered. 'What are you up to now?'

'Gabriella, it was my pleasure helping Elodie to arrange this celebration for you but birthday teas need cake and... here comes yours,' Philippe said, watching as a cake with seven lit candles was carried carefully in and placed in front of Gabby.

Philippe pushed his chair back, stood up and cleared his throat, and tapped his glass to get everyone's attention.

'A toast to Gabriella, a new friend whom I feel I've known forever. Happy Birthday and may the coming year bring you everything you hope for. Gabriella.'

'Gabriella,' chorused everyone.

'Now, blow out your candles,' Philippe said. 'Before they drip onto the cake. But don't forget to wish.' And he held her gaze for several seconds.

Gabriella took a deep breath and blew all seven candles out in one go, noting as she did so the way her name and the figure 70 was iced in white across the chocolate glaze. The waiter quickly scooped up the cake and took it away. Moments later, he returned and placed a perfect slice of Gâteau Opéra in front of everyone. Three layers of almond sponge cake, soaked in Grand Marnier, layered with ganache and coffee French buttercream with a chocolate glaze on top.

'Mmm. This is so good. I can't remember ever having a cake

anywhere as good as this before,' Gabby murmured, using her dessert fork to scrape up the last of the crumbs on her plate.

'I hoped you'd like it,' Philippe said. 'I will make it for you again next year.'

'You made it for me?'

Philippe nodded. 'Oui.'

Gabby leant and kissed him on the cheek. 'Thank you.'

Philippe fleetingly placed his hand over hers. 'The pleasure is all mine, Gabriella.'

Elodie had left the table and wandered over to look at the photographs of the Hôtel Le Provençal hanging on the wall. 'Was it like this when you worked there, Gabby? Or are they earlier? It looks a magnificent place. That grand staircase is so imposing.'

'Sadly, before my time. I think they're mainly late forties and very early fifties. Although the staircase was obviously still there when I worked there.'

'Such a shame it was left to rot for all those years,' Elodie said. 'Can you imagine how people today would love all that Art Deco and the history of the place?'

Gabby nodded. 'Yes, but times change, people's values and priorities change and they move on, and sadly we have to accept that.' She glanced across to where Harriet was talking with Jessica. 'Those two seem to be getting on well. I'm glad. Harriet will have a ready made friend when we all move down.'

It was gone six o'clock when Philippe suggested they should all make a move. Elodie and Harriet turned to go to the counter just inside the door to settle the bill but Philippe waylaid them.

'It's done,' he said quietly.

'But,' Elodie and Harriet uttered the word in unison.

'My birthday present for Gabriella,' Philippe said, his voice vetoing any argument.

'Thank you,' Elodie said. 'It was an especially lovely tea party.'

'I thank you too,' Harriet said.

The seven of them walked back to the apartment in a neatly divided group. Jessica linked her arm in Mickaël's on one side and Harriet was surprised when he offered her his other arm but laughingly accepted it. Elodie and Gazz walked behind them, and Philippe took Gabby's arm as he'd left his stick behind for that exact purpose. High spirited 'See you later' goodbyes were said all round when they reached the apartment block.

A little while later, having said goodbye to the Vincent family, the three of them were sitting out contentedly on the balcony relaxed and happy, looking down on the lights of Juan.

'I can't believe how much food we've eaten today,' Elodie said. 'I'm sure I've put on pounds this holiday. As for that amazing cake Philippe made. Definitely starting a diet on the fourth.' She looked at the other two. 'You don't think Jessica is going to feed us tonight as well, do you?'

Harriet laughed. 'I think she said something about nibbles and drinks when she invited me.'

'Give me half an hour and I'll walk to the hotel with you to collect your things,' Gabby said, stretching her legs out in front of her.

Harriet looked at her. 'What?'

'Do not look at me like that. There is no way you are leaving here at gone midnight and walking back to the hotel. You can stay here. We leave on the third – when is your ticket for?'

'Also the third,' Harriet said. 'Afternoon flight to Bristol.'

'That's the one we're on,' Gabby said. 'So that's settled. We'll go and collect your things and you can check out. You're spending the next two and a half days with us – a trial run of living together. No argument.'

In the end it was Elodie who went with her mother to check out of the hotel and collect her things as Gabby had decided to go and have a quick cat nap in her bedroom. When Harriet went to see if she was ready to leave she was fast asleep and Elodie offered to go with her instead. It was difficult to tell who was the more surprised – Elodie for offering or Harriet for accepting the company.

28

Christmas fairy lights were still strung around and between the trees lining their route and along various buildings and twinkled brightly as Elodie and Harriet made their way to Boulevard Édouard Baudoin and Harriet's hotel. Elodie stood for a moment, her back to the hotel, taking everything in – the lights, the sea, the moon, the salty air, before releasing a deep happy sigh.

'I love it here. I'm so glad Gabby has decided to return and I get to come and live here.'

'It's not always going to be Christmas time though,' Harriet said. 'Real life has a habit of switching the fairy lights off along with the illusion that life is perfect for everyone.'

Elodie turned to her. 'I know that, of course I do. But everything seems brighter, more vibrant down here somehow, especially when the sun shines. Don't you feel that?'

'I do like it here,' Harriet sighed. 'But it's not where I was expecting to live when I returned. As for the three of us moving in together, I just don't know whether that will work.'

'Why not? Three generations living together is quite common

in some countries. Taking care of each other. Like proper families do, so I guess it would be difficult for us.'

Harriet didn't respond to the sarcasm in her voice and they were both silent for several seconds.

'All I know is that I love the idea of a different life over here,' Elodie said. 'To be honest, I felt in a bit of a rut back in Devon and I can't see anything changing there but being here makes me feel alive once again.' She stole a quick glance at Harriet. 'If I tell you something you have to promise not to tell Gabby.'

'I promise.' Harriet said, a wary edge to her voice.

'You said the other day that I wouldn't know anything about being in a controlling relationship. And I don't, not to the same degree that you clearly suffered. A few months ago I finished a relationship with an old boyfriend. Mark and I were friends for a few years before we started a relationship. Everything was good at first but then he began to make suggestions as to what I should be doing, what I should wear, what he didn't like. He'd get a bit cross when I didn't always do what he wanted.'

'You didn't mention this to Gabby?'

'No. Then one evening I refused to do something and Mark slapped me across the face. He apologised immediately but that slap did me a favour. It brought me to my senses and I told him to get lost.'

Harriet exhaled. 'Good for you.'

'I daren't tell Gabby – she'd be furious. Probably march me off to the nearest police station to have him arrested for assault. Anyway,' Elodie shrugged. 'That's one of the reasons I love the idea of a new start down here.'

Never mind Gabby being furious about that boy, Harriet herself felt murderous towards him for hurting her daughter. 'I promise I won't mention this to Gabby as it's in the past, but you must also promise me something. That you will at least think about talking to me if you have a problem in the future.'

'You're definitely going to be around then?' Elodie gave her a challenging look.

'Yes. I desperately want to do the right thing by you. I know I can't change the past but I can do better in the future.' Harriet paused as they turned to enter the hotel and she pushed open the door before she added quietly. 'I know it's going to take time for you to come to terms with having me in your life but I can only promise to do my best and to be there whenever you need me.'

The receptionist glanced up as they entered.

'You found your mother then?' she asked, smiling at Elodie.

'Yes, I think I have, thank you,' Elodie answered, before turning to Harriet with a thoughtful look and giving her a smile that made Harriet's heart skip a beat as she realised Elodie had listened to her heart felt words and believed her.

* * *

The three of them spent the early part of the evening companionably in the apartment before making their way to the penthouse and the New Year's Eve Party. As they left, Gabby took the bottle of pink champagne out of the fridge and looked at Elodie.

'Shall we take this with us?'

'Good idea,' Elodie said.

Mickaël opened the door to them. 'Come on through. The others are the sitting room.'

Gabby handed him the champagne. 'A little contribution.'

'Thank you. We'll save it for the midnight toast.'

Elodie's heart had sank at the word 'others'. Gazz had told her as they walked back after the tea party that he was looking forward to seeing in the New Year with her, but did Mickaël's words mean Fiona was here? To her relief it was just the other three Vincent family members standing by a large terracotta pot, who greeted them. A large terracotta pot with not only a red bow tied around it, but a well established lemon tree with seven bright yellow fruit hanging from its branches, growing out of it.

'Happy Birthday again, Gabriella,' Jessica said. 'We couldn't bring your present to the restaurant for obvious reasons, but this is for your new home.'

'I don't know what to say,' Gabby said. 'Except thank you so much.' She reached out to touch the leaves and gently rubbed them between her fingers releasing a subtle scent of lemon.

'We'll keep it here out on the balcony and take care of it until you move in and then we'll bring it over to you.'

'Gabby makes the most delicious lemonade in the summer,' Elodie said. 'So with lemons in the garden it really is going to be homemade.'

'We'll look forward to that then,' Jessica said. 'Now, I'll just fetch the few nibbles I've organised while Mickaël and Gazz make sure you've all got a drink.'

'I'll give you a hand,' Harriet said, following her into the kitchen.

'How soon do you expect to be over here?' Mickaël asked as he handed drinks to Gabby and Philippe.

'Not sure. Could be a few weeks, or a couple of months. I suspect selling my house will take time. I think, realistically, it could be Easter before we move,' Gabby said.

'There's nothing to stop you coming over for a long weekend before is there?' Philippe said.

'In theory no, but probably in practice, yes,' Gabby said.

'I like the theory answer better,' Philippe said.

Gazz moved towards Elodie carrying two glasses of wine and handed her one. 'Santé,' he said as they clinked glasses.

'No Fiona tonight?' Elodie asked before she could stop herself.

Gazz shook his head. 'She's not talking to me at the moment. We had a row about me not joining her at her parents' tonight and then going on to a club with the others.' He shrugged. 'I'd rather be here with you and my own parents to be honest. Not a fan of nightclubs at the best of times and New Year's Eve is always a bit over the top,' Gazz took a sip of his wine. 'So, are you looking forward to getting back to Devon and starting to organise your move over here?'

Elodie nodded enthusiastically and accepted the change of conversation. Now wasn't the time, or the place, to press him on his relationship with Fiona, she was just happy he wanted to be here tonight.

'I am. The quicker I can return here the happier I shall be.'

'And Gabby?'

'She's looking forward to the three of us being reunited and all living under the same roof. Although Harriet still has her doubts I think, as I do, but we are seemingly united in this crazy adventure for Gabby.' Elodie looked across the room to where Gabby was laughing at something Philippe had said. 'I think Gabby's delight may also be bound up in getting to know your grandfather better.'

'You think?' Gazz smiled. 'I think that's his plan too.' He took a sip of his drink. 'You seem more relaxed around Harriet tonight.'

Elodie nodded thoughtfully. 'I suppose you could say we're definitely getting there.'

Harriet and Jessica appeared just then, and put a couple of plates of canapés on the table.

'A couple of hours ago I was thinking about going on a diet

and didn't think I could eat another thing after today's celebrations,' Elodie said. 'But these look delicious and I'm a bit hungry again. Besides, it would be rude not to, as your mum has gone to the trouble of making them.'

At five minutes to midnight, Jessica opened the balcony doors and carried champagne and glasses to the table out there. The night air was calm, the sky that curious dark but light colour due to the light pollution, making it all but impossible to see any stars, although the moon was silvery bright, down below, the lights along the Promenade du Soleil twinkled and car lights travelled along the bord du mer. With the television on in the background counting down the minutes, the seven of them stood on the wide balcony in a circle holding hands and as the last second of the old year disappeared, Mickaël was leading them in a rousing chorus of Auld Lang Sang. A moment later, as car horns down on the Promenade du Soleil were honked in jubilation and fireworks across the bay started, hugs were exchanged and the champagne poured.

Standing with his arm around Elodie's shoulders, watching the noisy effervescent coloured designs fizzing before fading away in the night sky, Gazz held her tight and whispered. 'Happy New Year, Elodie. I have a feeling it's going to be a great one for both of us.' And he gently kissed her cheek.

'Happy New Year to you, too. Good Luck with your new business,' she replied, before returning his cheek kiss, inwardly glad that he hadn't kissed her properly with everyone here. She hoped she still had that to look forward to sometime in the future.

Gabby, standing hand in hand with Philippe, breathed a happy sigh. She turned sideways to look at him. 'Happy New Year and thank you for one of the best birthdays ever.' Philippe smiled and squeezed her hand.

'Thank you for coming into my life,' he said quietly before gently giving her lips a fleeting kiss. 'I think you and I will have a very Happy New Year together.'

Mickaël, Jessica and Harriet had a mini group hug as they wished each other Happy New Year. Harriet smiled as her new friend, Jessica, and her husband kissed, whilst silently wondering whether she would ever have anyone special in her own life ever again. But even without a special person at her side she knew she was happier than she'd been for years. She glanced across affectionately at Gabby standing with Philippe and Elodie with Gazz and smiled. A few weeks ago she would never have entertained the idea that she would see in the New Year with her family, let alone be considering moving to France and living with them.

As the spectacle of the fireworks died away and the car horns grew quiet Philippe, with a wicked twinkle in his eye, suggested that the seven of them should make a joint New Year Resolution.

'That way if we break it someone will know and can push us back on track.'

'Papa,' Mickaël said, looking at him warily. 'How much have you had to drink? Nobody ever manages to keep resolutions beyond January sixth, Epiphany, if they last even that long. A joint one is impossible.'

'The resolution I'm proposing will be easy to keep, so raise your glasses,' Philippe said and he gazed at them, almost daring them not to join in. Bemused, everyone did as they were told.

'Right, repeat after me – This is the year we resolve to live our best lives and practise Carpe Diem – seize the day, every day.'

'See, that wasn't difficult, was it?' Philippe said after everybody had made their commitment to the resolution with determination in their voices.

It was an hour later when Gabby gathered Elodie and Harriet

to her side. 'Time for bed, I think?' And the three of them made their way over to Jessica and the others to thank them all for everything before saying their 'Goodnights', and making their way down to their own apartment.

29

'This has been one of the best birthdays and New Year celebrations of my life,' Gabby said, as they let themselves into the apartment. 'It's been a really special one. Thank you both.'

'Do you think that maybe Philippe has something to do with you feeling like that?' Harriet asked, smiling at her.

Gabby gave a nonchalant shrug but couldn't stop herself smiling back. 'Maybe. I'm certainly going to try and keep his resolution in mind. I hope the two of you will do the same.

'Anyone fancy joining me for a cup of hot chocolate?' Elodie said. 'I felt a bit cold out on the balcony after the fireworks.'

'Yes, please,' Gabby and Harriet said in unison.

A contented silence descended a few moments later as the three of them sat in the sitting room sipping their creamy drinks.

'I'm SO looking forward to moving down here,' Elodie said. 'It can't happen quickly enough for me.'

'I must admit I haven't felt this excited for the coming year for, oh, for ever really,' Gabby said quietly. 'And I have to say, I didn't expect to feel this level of exhilaration at the thought of moving back to Juan-les-Pins after all these years.'

'I think you're being very brave, Mum,' Harriet said. 'Selling up and moving is stressful at any age, let alone moving to another country.' She frowned and bit her lip, unwilling to say any more, to tell them just how worried she'd been about returning to the country of her birth. Only the thought of leaving the last twenty years behind and the hoped for reconciliation with both her mother and her daughter had given her the strength to push through the stress of those months.

Gabby nodded. 'But the thing is for me, I'm coming home. Something I never thought would happen.' She took a sip of her drink before looking at her daughter. 'I know Devon is the home you thought you were coming back to but I'm sure France will quickly become your and Elodie's home as well as mine. The three of us all living together in one place is a dream coming true for me.' She stood up.

'Now we'd better find the bed linen and get the bed settee made up. Jessica said there was extra in the cupboard when we arrived.'

'You get off to bed, Gabby,' Elodie said. 'I'll give Harriet a hand with the bed.'

'Okay. Night-night, you two. See you in the morning,' and Gabby blew them both a kiss before going to her room.

Harriet picked up the empty mugs. 'I'll put these in the dishwasher if you can find the bed stuff for me, please?'

Elodie nodded and moved towards the cupboard in the hallway, deep in thought. Harriet's words from earlier about how she couldn't change the past but that she would be better in the future dropped into her mind. She'd sounded so sincere and Elodie knew deep down that she simply couldn't carry on keeping her at arms' length. She too needed to make the effort to forget the past and concentrate on their future relationship, even though there were still things, feelings, that needed to be pulled out into the open, discussed and settled before they could be pushed down into their respective memory banks. But all that could wait until they were back in Devon, Elodie decided. She didn't want to spoil the memory of this first Christmas in France by delving into the dirt of the past here and spoiling her happy memories of the holiday. Far better to discuss and dissect things back in Dartmouth where Harriet's actions all those years ago had effectively changed all their lives.

Elodie opened the cupboard door and took out a couple of towels before returning to the sitting room and handing them to Harriet, who looked at her in surprise. 'Couldn't you find any bed linen?'

'I didn't look. Not sure how comfy the settee will be as a bed so why don't you sleep in the twin bed in my room. It's already made up.'

There was a couple of seconds silence before Harriet smiled. 'Thank you.'

'Be warned. You'll be on the settee tomorrow night if you snore,' Elodie said. 'I bag the bathroom first.' And she left Harriet to pick up her things from the side of the settee, feeling that finally she was beginning to get used to her mother being back in her life.

Half an hour later, Harriet lay in bed listening to her daughter's rhythmic breathing and thinking about the future. Six days ago she'd been worried about meeting up with both her mother and her daughter and now here they were, all three of them planning to embark on a new beginning together. One that would heal the past and hopefully create an unbreakable bond between them. Elodie might be insisting on calling her Harriet rather than Mum but with patience and time that could change.

Harriet snuggled down deeper under the duvet, happier than she'd ever expected to be again. Her last thought as she drifted off into a deep sleep was that Gabby and Elodie were right. This New Year was on course to be wonderful.

* * *

After leaving Harriet and Elodie, Gabby stood out on the balcony of her room for several moments, breathing in the salty air that was now tinged with gunpowder from the earlier fireworks. It had been a truly wonderful birthday, one that would stay with her forever. There was still too much light pollution to see any stars but the moon was shining brightly, its silvery light over the Hôtel Le Provençal giving the old Art Deco building an air of romance that was sadly missing during daylight hours these days.

Gabby remembered:

the way the building had majestically dominated the skyline of Juan-les-Pins for decades. Walking along the Promenade du Soleil or sunbathing on the beach, you couldn't fail to see the word Provencal proudly stretched across the top of it. Even in the sixties, when it was no longer revered as it had been in the twenties and thirties after it had given birth to a whole new era on the Côte d'Azur with its tennis club, private jetty and luxury rooms, she'd felt proud when she told people where she worked. The people she worked with were, in the main, friendly, she met the occasional famous person and most days, when she was still dreaming of reaching the dizzy heights of becoming the Hotel Concierge, she'd looked forward to going to work. Things had started to change when she'd realised, after a particularly unsavoury incident with the deputy manager, she'd never reach the dizzy heights of the top job, simply because she was a woman. The dream had been in the process of being permanently squashed by the male dominated workforce, at about the same time she became pregnant. Finding herself 'with child' as the hotel manager had witheringly described her condition, had brought the wrath of, not only her father, but the hotel management down on her head. Her dismissal had been instant. Christophe had remained unscathed by the scandal that had engulfed her simply because he was male and it was her fault for encouraging him. She'd naturally turned to him for help when she realised she was pregnant, but Christophe had accused her of trying to trap him into marriage and told her the problem was hers and hers alone. There was no doubt he'd used her. He'd had no intention of ever becoming a married family man. Being seen to date her was an attempt to hide the fact that he was gay. And he'd certainly succeeded in hiding that fact from her. Thank God so much had changed since the sixties.

A car horn blaring out on the bord de mer brought her out of reverie and Gabby started. Life had turned out so differently to the way she'd imagined in those far off days. Would she have done things differently if she could? Yes. Did she regret anything? Yes, unlike the song, she did have regrets. Regrets that mainly concerned Harriet. This holiday in France had been extra special for several reasons but one important reason stood out. Harriet had returned and was in her life once again. Gabby could only hope and pray that this New Year's Eve had heralded in a real year of unity in their fractured family and that their lives would now be forever entwined.

30

New Year's Day and Elodie was awake early. Not wanting to disturb Harriet, who was still in a deep sleep she got dressed quickly, deciding to shower after breakfast. She grabbed her jacket and purse and set off on the croissant run. The streets were quiet, the few people who were out all appeared to be clutching boulangerie bags and Elodie saw only the occasional car as she walked. When she got back with the still warm baguette and croissants Gabby and Harriet were in the kitchen, with their first coffee of the day. 'Breakfast on the balcony while we can?' Elodie asked, opening the French doors. 'The sky is blue and the sun is out.'

The three of them sat in companionable silence enjoying their breakfast. 'We won't have this view from the terrace of No.5,' Elodie said. 'But we'll be able to have a pre-breakfast swim if we want to.' She glanced at Harriet. There was so much to learn about her. Things that she would have known for years if life had been different.

'Do you swim?'

'No, not really. Having a pool though, might be just the incentive I need to start and get fit.'

'I'm definitely going to try and swim every day,' Elodie said. 'I think we should get a dog and a cat when we move into No.5.'

'A dog would be nice,' Harriet said. 'Remember Tess, Mum? I haven't had a dog since then.'

'Talking of No.5. I've got a name for the villa,' Elodie said, breaking off a piece of croissant.

Gabby looked at her. 'And?'

'I think we should call it Villa de L'Espoir – Villa of Hope. What d'you think? We're all full of hope for the future, aren't we?'

Harriet smiled. 'I like it. Mum?

Gabby nodded. 'Yes. Villa de L'espoir. Very apt.'

'That's settled then, no more calling it No.5,' Elodie said. 'If it's okay with you two, today I'm planning on working on the laptop, sorting out my journal, writing a To Do list for when we get back and drafting a few emails to editors. That resolution Philippe made us all make last night was a good one. I am determined to write more of the things I want to write and to try and live my best life. I also need to try to figure out how to get everything back in my suitcase.'

'Fancy joining me for a walk?' Gabby asked, looking at Harriet.

'As long as it's not one of your marathons,' Harriet said. 'A gentle stroll with you around Juan-les-Pins would be lovely.'

Elodie stood up. 'I'll see you both later then.'

Harriet looked at her mum as Elodie disappeared in the direction of her room. 'You did a brilliant job bringing her up. I doubt I would have done so well. Thank you for being there for her,' she said quietly.

'She's always missed you, even when she got angry with you when she was a teenager. She coped by not letting herself think about you or reply to the cards you sent. It's good to see the pair of you together finally,' Gabby said.

'I'm sorry for not coming on Christmas Day. I was scared of ruining things, scared of Elodie's reaction.'

'I was disappointed, I admit. Elodie was really upset with me when I laid a place for you at the table, so I think you were probably right. The day is always an emotional one for most people. Everyone has such high expectations of it being wonderful but it rarely meets all those expectations.'

Gabby stood up.

'Come on. Let's clear the breakfast things away and go for that walk.'

Walking through Juan the two of them chatted away in a manner that made both of them secretly sad, remembering the lost years.

'I know I thanked everybody yesterday for the wonderful birthday but one of the best parts was having you there after all these years,' Gabby said, squeezing Harriet's arm. 'Thank you – and thank you too, for agreeing to move to France with us.'

Harriet sighed and chose her words carefully. The last thing she wanted to do was upset Gabby.

'To be honest, I'm still hesitant about that. Not moving to France but all of us living together. I'm not sure that I shouldn't buy my own place. Be independent for once. Work out how I want to live my life in the future,' she paused. 'I know it sounds a bit precious, but I need to find myself again. I've realised that Todd did a real job on me and my self esteem.'

Gabby didn't answer, she simply indicated they needed to cross the street and turn left under the archway with Brocante/Antiquities painted on a wooden sign nailed to it.

'Is this where Elodie found your birthday present?'

'Yes. I wanted to see it again.'

Gabby stood on the gravel path looking at the bicycle with its basket of hyacinths next to the closed shop door and its Fermé sign hanging from a catch in the middle of the wood.

'Colette used to ride a bike like that everywhere,' Gabby said, smiling at the memory. 'It was painted in those colours too. I remember racing her along Cap d'Antibes on our days off. She always beat me.' Gabby bent to take a closer look at the frame of the bike. 'The serial number was on a piece of metal between the frame of the bike and the seat. Colette's bike had a very memorable one. It was all twos.' She squinted at the area just under the seat. 'I can just make it out and I do believe it's her old bike, number twenty-two thousand, two hundred and twenty-two.' She straightened up. 'How amazing is that? Colette would love the idea that her precious bike was now a plant holder.'

'Shame the place isn't open today,' Harriet said. 'Elodie did say we'd find lots of bits and pieces here when we move down. I look forward to having a good old rummage in there. Come on, let's get back to our walk.'

They turned and made their way up the gravel path, under the arch and out into the street.

'Elodie is so excited about moving into Villa de L'Espoir,' Harriet said, remembering to give the villa its chosen name.

Gabby gave her a quick look. 'Yes, she is. And that is one major reason for you to live with us. You'll both benefit from establishing a mother daughter relationship by living in the same house, even if it is a bit late in the day. Living with Elodie will remind you of the woman you were when you gave birth to her, which will help you find yourself as a person again.'

Harriet was silent.

'Please think about it. I think being surrounded by family love is the best way to recover from emotional trauma. I'm not saying we're all going to live in harmony every day because the chances are we won't, none of us are perfect. But moving here, all three of us living together, does at least give us a chance of growing closer.'

By lunch time, when the others returned, Elodie was pleased with her morning's work. She'd planned out a series of features as well as several single ones, she'd researched the names of magazine editors and half a dozen e-mails to editors had been drafted. The brochures she'd collected from the Tourist Office over the last few weeks were all organised and in a large envelope, when she got home she'd scan them into her computer.

There were also days marked out in her new diary for doing her own writing, and she'd got the bones of a short story down. All in all, a good morning's work. She'd even pulled her suitcase out of the bottom of the wardrobe, put it on the floor by her bed and half heartedly placed a few things inside before zipping it up and replacing it in the wardrobe. Tomorrow would be soon enough to pack.

When Gabby and Harriet returned the three of them enjoyed what Gabby always called an 'eat up the fridge' lunch. Talk was all about plans for the future and the hopes they all had for this New Year. When Harriet said that once back in Bristol she'd cancel her rental agreement and move down to Devon to help with everything that would need doing before they moved to France, Gabby released a sigh of relief. Only for it to be short lived when Harriet added she was still thinking about where to live when they moved to France.

31

Everyone was rather subdued the following morning, realising the holiday was truly nearing its end. Together, the three of them took down the fairy lights and dismantled the Christmas trees putting everything back in the boxes they'd bought them in. Elodie took the throw off the settee and folded it up ready to put at the bottom of her suitcase. She was planning to put everything else on top in the hope it would squash down. She stopped packing and went to find the others in the sitting room.

'You know we'd decided we'd leave the decorations here?'

Gabby nodded. 'Yes.'

'Why don't we leave them in Villa de L'Espoir instead? Then they'd be over here ready and waiting for our first Christmas in the villa. Jessica probably doesn't need any more decorations anyway.'

'Good idea,' Gabby said. 'Let's stop for coffee now and you and Harriet can take them to the villa afterwards.'

An hour later, as Elodie pressed the remote and the electric gates of Villa L'Espoir swung open, Harriet took a deep breath. Gabby extolling the virtues of them all living together and the way it would help them to grow closer again was one thing but did Elodie feel the same?

It wasn't until they'd placed the decorations in the understairs cupboard and had opened one of the French doors to wander out into the garden for a few moments though, that Harriet broached the subject.

'I've told Gabby that I'm not sure about us all living together under one roof. I think it would be better for me to find a place of my own and leave the two of you here. We'd still see a lot of each other but we wouldn't be under one another's feet.'

'What did Gabby say?'

'Insists that living together would be the best thing for us all to bond properly.'

Elodie was silent for several seconds before she shrugged. 'Maybe she's right. You can always move out to your own place if it doesn't work and the three of us find ourselves moaning and grousing about each other. At least we'd have tried then.'

Harriet nodded. 'Okay, I'll move in with you both on a three month trial, if it doesn't work I'll find my own place close by. Just don't mention the phrase 'trial period' to Gabby.' She glanced around at the neglected garden. 'Do you like gardening?'

Elodie shook her head. 'Not much. Gabby does though. Do you?'

Harriet nodded. 'Yes. I look forward to helping Gabby get this garden back up to scratch,' and she absently pulled some weeds out from around a mimosa tree whose vibrant yellow balls of flowers were beginning to burst open in clusters.

'We'd better lock up the villa and get back to finish tidying up,' Elodie said as a picture of her mother and grandmother working together in the garden sprang into her mind. The two of them having a common interest would help heal their broken relationship. She couldn't help wondering though, what it was going to take to fully mend her own emotional connection with her mother.

Back at the apartment that afternoon they were just gearing themselves up to tackle the vacuuming, and making sure the kitchen and the bathroom were clean, when there was a knock at the door.

Elodie was surprised to see Gazz when she went through to open it.

'I have messages for everyone from on high,' he said.

'You'd better come in then and deliver them,' Elodie said, laughing.

'Have you planned anything for your last evening?' Gazz asked, looking at them. They shook their heads.

'No, we were just planning on a quiet evening, maybe a last walk along the Promenade du Soleil,' Gabby said.

'Gabby, Philippe would like you to have supper with him. Half past seven for eight o'clock upstairs. Can I tell him you said yes?'

'Of course,' Gabby said, smiling.

'Elodie, I thought maybe you'd like to have another scooter ride and afterwards I could buy you supper in Antibes old town? Would that be okay with you?' He looked at her anxiously.

Elodie nodded. 'Perfect. Thank you.'

'See you outside at seven thirty then.'

Gazz turned to Harriet. 'Dad has a couple of friends coming to watch a big football match and my mother is hoping, as you'll be alone for the evening, that she can escape with a bottle of Prosecco and keep you company down here for a couple of hours?'

'Your mum is very welcome to join me with or without Prosecco,' Harriet said.

The rest of the day flew by as the three of them did their chores, shared another fridge lunch of odds and ends, and went for a final walk along the Promenade du Soleil before returning

to the apartment to get ready for their last evening of the
holiday.

* * *

Elodie met Gazz outside the apartment block at seven-thirty
promptly. He greeted her with two cheek kisses before handing
her the usual helmet and bending to check the strap for her.

'I thought we'd have a wander around the old harbour in
Antibes before dinner. I've booked a table for eight-fifteen.'

'Sounds good. Not too posh a place, I hope. I've only got
jeans on.'

'You're fine. Hop on then and we'll be off.'

Minutes later, Elodie had her arms around Gazz's waist and
they were speeding around the Cap d'Antibes. She was definitely
getting better at this scooter lark and she relaxed more and found
herself enjoying the ride. As they rounded the bend by the
Restaurant de Bâcon she turned her head and had a clear view
across the water towards the lights of Nice airport on the other
side of the bay. It was too dark to see the snow capped Alps that
she knew towered above the airport. Elodie twisted her head back
again. She didn't want to think about the airport tonight. Only
another eighteen hours and she'd be there, in the departure
lounge, getting ready to leave France.

Gazz parked the scooter in a designated parking space near
the market and they wandered hand in hand down towards the
old harbour. The Christmas lights were still switched on, an
accordionist was moving slowly between the bars, restaurants
and little cafés that lined the street, and to Elodie it felt like one
jolly street party was being held. Down by the old harbour they
turned right and walked alongside the moored boats, mainly

motor cruisers with the occasional sailing yacht squeezed in between them.

'Do you sail?' Gazz asked her, as they stopped to admire an old fashioned wooden sailing boat.

'A little. We live near a river so there are a lot of boats around but I've only ever been crew on dinghies. Do you?'

'As often as I can. If the business takes off, I hope to be able to buy a small sailing sloop in a couple of years. In the meantime, I crew for friends whenever they'll have me. This summer I will be busy so I don't expect to have a lot of free time to go sailing.' He glanced at his watch. 'We return now and make for the restaurant.'

The restaurant Gazz led Elodie to was one of several on a street which had a wide pavement area in front of it with tables and benches but they were shown inside to a table near the back by a log fire. Christmas decorations were still in evidence and Elodie was relieved to see several women dressed for comfort rather than fashion. Gazz ordered a non-alcoholic beer for himself and Elodie asked for a glass of red wine while they studied the extensive menu.

Once they'd chosen a main course each, steak haché and frites for Gazz and maigret du canard with dauphinoise potatoes for Elodie – neither of them felt hungry enough for a starter – Elodie took a sip of her wine.

'When do you return to Paris?'

'Tomorrow evening,' Gazz said. 'Just for a final week. Tying things up at work and clearing my apartment out. Then I'll be back down here to get ready for the summer.'

'Has Jessica come round to the idea of your new business? She didn't seem too keen before Christmas.' And Fiona definitely wasn't, Elodie thought.

'Mum is a bit torn, I think. She's looking forward to me living back down here but worries that I've taken a gamble too far on a risky business.' He grinned at Elodie. 'Which may well turn out to be true but I'm not admitting that to her until I've given it my best shot.'

'What about Fiona?' Elodie asked quietly. 'She didn't seem to like her boyfriend stepping off the career ladder either.' Elodie knew Gazz and Fiona's relationship was none of her business but she didn't want to leave tomorrow, even dreaming for one moment that when she returned she and Gazz might become a couple, if this was impossible. She knew that he liked her because he had told her so but she needed to know where Fiona stood in his affections. She was pretty sure Gazz wasn't the type to two-time his girlfriend. Elodie tried not to smile thinking how his mother would react to him doing that. There was no way Jessica would let him get away with that kind of behaviour.

Gazz reached out for her hand.

'Fiona and I have been friends for years, generally going around with the same gang of friends but we're not and never have been in a relationship although I know she wanted us to be. I sensed she was trying to imply to you that we are.'

Elodie nodded, remembering the possessive hand on his arm. 'Yes, she definitely was.'

Gazz glanced at her. 'We rowed about that the other evening when I told her to stop implying things that weren't true. I hope our friendship will survive but Fiona can be difficult when she doesn't get her own way. She's starting a new job in Monaco this week. I'm hoping she will meet someone who will sweep her off her feet. Someone with a proper career plan and a bigger bank balance than me.' Their food arrived at that moment and Gazz released her hand as the waiter placed their meals in front of them, wishing them 'Bon appétit.'

As the waiter left them, Gazz took hold of her hand again.

'There is one thing I am certain about though. Whatever Fiona hoped to happen between her and me, is even more impossible now that I've met you. I'm so happy you came here for Christmas and I'll be waiting and counting the days until you return.'

* * *

Gabby was in her room getting ready to have supper in the penthouse with Philippe. She'd left the only dressy dress she'd brought with her hanging in the bathroom as she showered, hoping the steam would refresh it. If she'd known they were going to have such a full social life while they were here she'd have packed another one or two. Thinking of packing, she glanced at the open suitcase on the other bed where she'd half-heartedly packed a few things. The Hôtel Le Provencal ashtray was sitting on top of everything for the moment. She'd forgotten to put it with the things Elodie and Harriet had taken to the villa. It was very heavy, hopefully it wouldn't push her case over the weight limit. Gabby crossed over to it and picked it up, her thoughts going back to the days when it had been commonplace item in her life.

Strange how such an ordinary every day item, once viewed as a necessity everywhere, had become a symbol of an anti-social habit. She'd hated them on the reception desk. Horrible dirty things. She'd had to tolerate them though, otherwise people just threw the dog ends everywhere, some even stamped them out on the marble in front of the desk. Gabby had been glad it wasn't her job to clean them. Her finger traced the lettering in the bowl of the tray. There had been three sizes, she remembered: small for bedside tables, medium for the reception desk and large for the bar areas. The large ones, which were deeper than the smaller ashtrays, had frequently been broken by inebriated guests accidentally sending them flying. Elodie had been lucky to find one of the large ones in such pristine condition.

Strange too, how such a previously hated object from the past had become something that she would treasure going into the future. She knew she would only have to look at it on the dresser Elodie wanted in the kitchen of the villa to be transported right back to the reception desk in the Hôtel Le Provençal. She'd adored organising the bookings in the huge ledger, welcoming the guests, making sure they were comfortable, organising tickets for concerts and keeping on top of the hundred and one jobs that came her way. It had been one of the happiest times of her life working there. The way it had ended though, suddenly and with disgrace, had almost finished her.

Gabby put the dish down on the dressing table. She'd take it up to show Philippe when she went for supper and ask him to keep it safe for her return. No point in taking it back only to have to pack it up again when they moved down.

Philippe was waiting for her when she stepped out of the lift in front of the penthouse and greeted her with a kiss on each cheek before looking at the ashtray with a quizzical expression.

'Elodie gave me this as part of my birthday present,' Gabby said. 'We decided to leave the Christmas decorations at the villa rather than in the apartment because I'm sure Jessica doesn't need them. Elodie and Harriet took them round earlier but I forgot to give them this. Would you keep it here for me? Seems silly taking it back only to return with it in a few months. And, to be honest, it's quite heavy and I'm wondering about the weight allowance of my case for the plane.'

'Elodie was a clever girl to find this for you. Of course I'll keep it safe,' Philippe promised when she handed it to him. 'It will stay in full view in my room to reassure myself that you are coming back to collect it. That you won't change your mind about moving here.'

Gabby shook her head. 'No, I won't change my mind. I'm as excited as Elodie, to be honest, but there is an awful lot to do.'

'Bon! Come on through to my sitting room. I have news to tell you over supper.'

Philippe had decided on a casual supper – chicken soup followed by a selection of cold meats with a green salad. No cheese but a slice of tarte tatin finished off the meal. All accompanied by a bottle of white burgundy.

'Thank you, Philippe, that was delicious,' Gabby said, smiling at him.

'My pleasure. I don't spend enough time in the kitchen these days. Jessica does the cooking for all of us. I just have to turn up at the table. It's good to have someone special to feed. I look forward to cooking you more meals very soon.'

'Talking of meals. The girls told me you insisted on paying the restaurant for that wonderful birthday tea, thank you. We've only known each other for such a short time but you've spoilt me more than I've been spoilt since I was a little girl. I wish I'd been able to reciprocate with at least a Christmas present. I shall find and bring you something special from Devon when I return.'

'Gabriella, I have no need of presents, the only thing I find myself hoping for and wanting, is you in my life.' Philippe reached out and took her hand. 'You make me feel alive again. I am impatient for the day you return and we can see each other every day. I hope you have the same feeling.' He gave her a searching look as he waited for her response.

'I can't quite believe how I do feel about you to be honest,' Gabby confessed. 'Like you said at the tea party, we are new friends but it feels like we've always known each other.' She paused. 'It's been a long time since I had a man in my life who makes me feel like you do. I'm looking forward so much to returning and knowing you are waiting for me makes my heart beat that bit faster.'

Philippe raised her hand to his lips and placed a gentle kiss on the back of it.

'You said you had some news to tell me?' Gabby said. 'I hope it's good news?'

'Everyone, they return to work today, so I make a few enquiries with a contact or two at the mairie. My first bit of news is that work will recommence at the Hôtel Le Provençal this very week. The difficulties have been overcome and soon the final stage of conversion to apartments will be finished.'

'That's good news. I've hated seeing it so neglected and all the hoarding surrounding it.'

Philippe topped up her wine glass. 'My other news concerns Jean-Frances Moulin. There is a strip of land behind No.5, yes? About half a hectare?'

'Yes. I'd forgotten it came with the villa. I'd guess it's pretty over grown these days. I remember my mother keeping a few chickens and occasionally there would be a pig in the old shed. I always wanted a pony to live in the field but was never allowed one. There is probably still a gate in the back hedge for access.'

'It's the land that Moulin wanted as much as the villa. He planned on demolishing No.5 and building three or four new villas on the whole site. He'd even got tentative planning permission.'

'Without owning it?'

Philippe shrugged. 'It is possible.'

Philippe broke the short silence that sprung up between them as Gabby thought about the information he'd given her.

'You, of course, can apply to do the same legitimately and you would become a wealthy woman.'

Gabby rubbed her hand across her face. 'No, I wouldn't and I couldn't ever do that for several reasons. The villa and the cul-de-sac are perfect the way it was designed. There was always a neighbourly feeling about it and I hope when we move back, I will discover it is still the same – despite all the electric gates. Another reason I wouldn't knock down the villa and build all over the field is, I have no desire to be a wealthy woman.'

She took a deep breath. She'd trust Philippe with her life so she'd tell him the truth. 'The third reason is, it's not mine to sell. I made it over to Elodie as soon as I inherited it. I'm just the caretaker, really. The rent money down the years has gone into a trust account for her.' Gabby bit her lip. 'Nobody else knows about the house, although I did finally tell Elodie about the trust account the first time I took her to see No.5 but she doesn't know she is the legal owner of the villa. And, so far, I don't see any reason to tell her. The truth will all come out in good time.'

'Gabriella, thank you for trusting me with that information. I promise you, I too, will stay silent until you decide the time is right for Elodie to learn the truth.'

'Thank you,' Gabby said gratefully. 'Incidentally, we've decided to give the villa a name as well as a number. Elodie came up with Villa de L'Espoir which we decided was quite perfect.'

'I love the thought of the three of you starting new lives in the Villa of Hope. It is indeed a name parfait,' Philippe said.

Harriet had been alone in the apartment for less than five minutes before Jessica arrived holding the promised bottle of Prosecco.

'I hope you didn't mind me inviting myself,' said Jessica, twisting the cork and pouring two glasses. 'But there is only so much male rugby testosterone I can take. They always have a sense of humour failure too, when I tell them to calm down it's only a game.' She held out a glass to Harriet.

Harriet laughed as the two of them clinked glasses. 'Shame on you. You know how seriously men take their sport.'

'Do you have a sports mad man in your life?' Jessica said, sipping her drink and looking at Harriet over the brim.

Harriet stiffened before shaking her head. She'd expected that Gabby would have told Philippe about her situation and he would have passed it on to Jessica. But that clearly hadn't happened. 'I'm a widow. Todd, my husband, died several months ago.'

Jessica looked stricken. 'I'm so sorry. Mickaël is always telling me I ask too many questions.'

'It's fine.' Harriet bit her lip before glancing at Jessica. She sensed that the two of them were going to be good friends in the future. She didn't intend to talk about her marriage to everyone, some things were best forgotten in this new life of hers, but maybe it would be good to have someone, apart from Gabby, who knew the truth and could talk her out of the despondency that engulfed her when she thought about the mistake she made and her wasted life.

'It wasn't a happy marriage. Todd was a control freak. When someone is very ill and dies people say it was a happy release for them. I'm ashamed to say that Todd dying was a happy release for me.'

'Honest, not ashamed,' Jessica said robustly. 'It's sad but some horrible people simply do not deserve to be mourned when they die – whatever society might say about forgiveness.'

Harriet swallowed hard in an effort to stop the tears that were threatening. 'Thank you. My mother has been incredibly kind and understanding but not to be judged by a friend is a relief.'

There was a brief pause before Jessica spoke, moving the

conversation on. 'Do you have any plans for when you move down? Are you looking to work?'

'I haven't worked for the last twenty odd years,' admitted Harriet. 'Todd didn't allow me to work or have any independent interests. I doubt I have any employable skills, especially here in France when my French is so rusty. Gabby is keen for me to start painting again but,' she shrugged. 'Gabby and Elodie both tell me I haven't lost my touch but what I have lost is my confidence.'

'I don't suppose you have anything here you can show me?' Jessica asked.

'Only my new sketchbook which has a few sketches and doodles in it.' Harriet picked it up off the table where she'd left it and handed it to Jessica. While she turned the pages, Harriet topped up their glasses and waited.

'I love that picture of Elodie on the beach,' Jessica said closing the sketchbook and handing it back. 'I have a friend who owns one of the galleries in Antibes. When you return, I shall introduce you to Harry and I can't imagine him not wanting to show your work.'

'I haven't got anything to show him,' Harriet protested.

'Well, in between helping Gabby and Elodie pack up to move, get painting,' Jessica said. 'You, my new friend, will be the toast of the town this time next year, if I can have anything to do with it. Santé.'

'Santé,' a bemused Harriet echoed. Perhaps the gods would finally smile on her this year.

32

Gabby was putting the final few things in her case the next morning when she glanced out of window and saw two expensive cars park and half a dozen men in suits get out. Several builders' trucks were already parked up on site and Gabby could see workmen swarming over the scaffolding that covered the fabric of the building. Philippe was right. Work was starting again on the Hôtel Le Provençal.

Gabby watched as the men put on the hard white building regulation hats, before striding importantly here, there and everywhere clutching their clipboards. She was tempted to run down and ask if she, an old employee, could have a look around inside but decided against it. She'd keep her memories of the way it was on the day she left all those years ago. The hotel may have been far from perfect then, but she didn't want to see the total devastation that had since taken place inside.

The day Gabby had left the hotel forever she'd gone to say goodbye to a few people she would miss. Old Henri was one. Old Henri who had to be the oldest bellboy in the business and should have been pensioned off years ago, was forever moaning that the place was going to rack and to ruin. Although if half of what he muttered about the hotel's glamorous past was true, there was a different history hidden behind all the luxury, glitz and Art Deco.

'Not going to get the likes of Josephine (Baker), Marilyn (Monroe) or Maurice (Chevalier) coming here again, the state the place is in. Did I ever tell you about...' and he'd be off reminiscing. 'Today's swinging sixties lot think they invented free love. Huh, the Goulds could give them a lesson or two, especially her. Neither of them cared a fig about their marriage vows. You know what her favourite saying was? 'Money doesn't care who it belongs to'. For her everything revolved around money. She was a bad 'un through and through. Someone once said, "Mad, bad and dangerous to know," about her – and that sums her up. Got up to no good during the war too, up in Paris with the Nazis. Rumour says it was their money that repaired the hotel after it was bombed. Couldn't sell this place quick enough after Frank died.'

He'd nodded at her, his rheumy eyes looking at her sadly. 'Reckon you're right to be off. No future here for the likes of you.' He'd sighed before launching once again into the tale of Ella Fitzgerald opening her bedroom window and giving an impromptu performance to the people in the gardens. 'Those were the days,' he'd said over his shoulder as he was summoned to the reception desk to move a guest's luggage.

Gabby had turned away sadly and left. If only he knew how much she was going to miss this place despite its run-down appearance and its secret, if somewhat dubious, history. She dreaded to think what her own future might hold in store for her. Some people, her own father included, had already written her off as a lost cause.

Gabby zipped her case closed. The Hôtel Le Provençal hadn't been the only thing she'd missed during those first difficult months in England. She'd missed her mum, her friends, particularly Colette, she'd cried herself to sleep on many nights wishing she was still in France. In a way it had been a huge relief when she miscarried the baby that had been the reason to run as far as possible away from everything and everybody. But there had been no turning the clock back as far as her father was concerned. She'd brought shame on him and was not welcome back in his life. But her life had slowly moved on and she settled into a foreign English life. Meeting and marrying Eric, having Harriet, those had been the really good years. And then Eric had his heart attack and died, Elodie had been born and three years later Harriet had disappeared. Those had been the truly hard years.

Life was about to turn full circle though. Tonight she and Elodie would be back in Devon, whilst Harriet would be up in Bristol and the three of them would be kick starting plans for them all to move into Villa de L'Espoir.

'Taxi will be here soon, Gabby,' Elodie called out. 'Need a hand with your suitcase?'

'No, don't worry, I can manage. Thanks.'

Jessica had come down to say goodbye to them and to thank them for leaving the apartment so clean and tidy. 'I hope all our guests are as good as you, although I doubt anyone will become friends in the way you all have. I can't wait for you to be living down here permanently.'

'Taxi is here,' Philippe said, opening the door and looking in. 'Gabriella, I'll take your case.'

'With your new hip? No, you will not,' Jessica said. 'Gazz, you take Gabriella's case.'

Behind her back Philippe pulled a face which made everyone laugh and then Mickaël closed the apartment door behind them as they all made their way to the lift.

'I can't believe you've all come to see us off,' Gabby said.

'And we will all be here to welcome you back,' Philippe said, holding her hand tightly and kissing her cheek before she got into the taxi.

Gazz gave Elodie a tight hug and a quick kiss on the cheek

before she and Harriet cheek kissed everyone else, with Philippe whispering to Elodie, 'Look after Gabriella for me,' before she went to follow Harriet into the taxi. She turned back to look at Gazz just before she got in and saw him standing watching her with an unfathomable look on his face. Their eyes locked and for a few seconds everything and everyone melted into the background. The intensity in his eyes matched her own and Elodie knew that Gazz would be here waiting for her when she returned.

The three of them were finally in the taxi, the door was slammed shut and with a final wave they were on their way to Nice airport.

* * *

Once they'd checked in they went through to Duty Free with Elodie determined to treat herself to some new makeup and a bottle of her favourite perfume. As they browsed the counters Elodie looked at Gabby and Harriet and smiled to herself.

Both Gabby and Harriet raised her eyebrows at her.

'Are you going to share the joke?' Gabby asked.

Elodie glanced at Harriet, wondering how she would take what she was about to say.

'It's not really a joke. People go into Duty Free to buy stuff they maybe wouldn't normally buy and also to buy things they want to buy a little bit cheaper – like we are doing. And some people buy a special memento of their holiday as well, which we don't need to do.'

Gabby sighed. 'Where are you going with this? Do you want us to buy something special to remind us all of what happened this holiday?'

Elodie shook her head. 'No. It just occurred to me that under a month ago, the two of us arrived in France. Now we're leaving as a threesome with our own souvenir, Harriet, whose presence will constantly remind us of this Christmas.'

Both Gabby and Harriet laughed as Elodie moved away to find her favourite perfume.

'Elodie was right,' Gabby said, turning to Harriet. 'You are the Christmas present that tops all Christmas presents – and not one I dared to hope for.'

'You're not alone there,' Harriet said quietly, before giving her mother a tight hug. 'I can't believe I've found and been accepted back into the family fold by you.'

By the time they left Duty Free, the three of them had a clutch of carrier bags filled with wine, perfume and makeup.

Gabby and Elodie were seated together while Harriet was four or five rows in front. With their duty free stored safely in the overhead locker, both Elodie and Gabby fastened their safety belts.

Gabby sat back happily in her seat. From what Elodie had said in Duty Free, it sounded as though she was beginning to accept her mother's presence in her life. She knew Elodie had a lot of as yet unasked questions she would want the answers to, but hopefully given time, the two of them would re-connect as the mother and daughter they were.

As the plane began to taxi down the runway ready for take-off, Gabby looked out at the sparkling Mediterranean. Who would have believed that in less than a month their lives would have started to change so dramatically because of her desire to spend Christmas and her birthday in her home town? Even more unexpected was the fact that in a few more weeks she would once again be calling Antibes Juan-les-Pins home – and this time she would have the pleasure of being accompanied by both her daughter and her granddaughter. Not to mention the lovely

Philippe who wanted to be a part of her life as much as she wanted to be in his.

Thinking about the way Elodie had looked at Gazz as they left, she guessed that she too, had found a possible new love. Harriet, now part of the family again, had started the process of rediscovering who she was and hopefully she too, in the fullness of time, would find happiness.

As the plane rose into the air Gabby gave a sigh of contentment. It had certainly proved to be an unforgettable festive season. As for the future, it was impossible to know how everything would work out, she could only hope and pray for the best. She knew though, that despite all the worry about whether she was doing the right thing, she had been right to return to Antibes Juan-les-Pins.

She'd banished the ghosts of the past and even some of the present, now she had so much to look forward to in the future. Life was good and she, Gabriella Jacques, was looking forward to returning and living permanently in her hometown with her family around her.

ACKNOWLEDGMENTS

As always, my thanks go to Caroline Ridding at Boldwood Books for being such a wonderful editor – without her input and wise advice this novella would never have seen the light of day. Thanks also to the wider Boldwood Team, Amanda, Nia, Rose, and everyone else involved behind the scenes. To all my fellow Boldwood authors who are such a supportive bunch of people, thank you.

Thanks to Rachel Gilbey and her team of bloggers who support and help promote so many of us by spreading the word about our books.

And a grateful thanks to all my readers who make it all worthwhile.

Love

Jennie

AUTHOR NOTE

There really is a Hôtel Le Provençal in Antibes Juan-les-Pins that has been left derelict and run down since the late 1970s. In its heyday it epitomised the glamour and the glitz of the French Riviera. Several developers have begun to renovate the shell of the building during the last thirty years or so only to fall by the wayside as money ran out. But a few years ago the site was sold again and this time work has continued to turn the remnants of the ancient hotel into a block of luxurious apartments for today's celebrities and jet setters.

MORE FROM JENNIFER BOHNET

We hope you enjoyed reading *Christmas On The Riviera*. If you did, please leave a review.

If you'd like to gift a copy, this book is also available as an ebook, digital audio download and audiobook CD.

Sign up to Jennifer Bohnet's mailing list for news, competitions and updates on future books.

http://bit.ly/JenniferBohnetNewsletter

Explore more gloriously escapist reads from Jennifer Bohnet.

 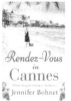

ABOUT THE AUTHOR

Jennifer Bohnet is the bestselling author of over 10 women's fiction novels, including *Villa of Sun and Secrets* and *The Little Kiosk By The Sea*. She is originally from the West Country but now lives in the wilds of rural Brittany, France.

Visit Jennifer's website: http://www.jenniferbohnet.com/

Follow Jennifer on social media:

facebook.com/Jennifer-Bohnet-170217789709356

twitter.com/jenniewriter

instagram.com/jenniebohnet

bookbub.com/authors/jennifer-bohnet

Boldwood

Boldwood Books is an award-winning fiction publishing company seeking out the best stories from around the world.

Find out more at www.boldwoodbooks.com

Join our reader community for brilliant books, competitions and offers!

Follow us
@BoldwoodBooks
@BookandTonic

Sign up to our weekly deals newsletter

https://bit.ly/BoldwoodBNewsletter

Printed in Great Britain
by Amazon

16232367R00122